MW00716105

THE WHITE HAND

a RUTHERFORD MANOR novel

Written by: Konn Lavery
Edited by: Robin Schroffel

MATRIX PRESSWORX

A division of Internet Matrix Inc.

© 2019 by Internet Matrix Inc. and Konn Lavery. All rights reserved.
Find out more at:
www.rutherford-manor.com
www.konnlavery.com

Published in Canada by Matrix Pressworx, A Division of Internet Matrix Inc.
No part of this publication may be reproduced, distributed, or transmitted
in any form or by any means, or stored in a database or retrieval system,
without the prior written permission of the publishers.

This is a work of fiction, names, characters, places and incidents either
are the result of the author's creative exploration or are used only in a
fictional manor. Any resemblance to actual persons, living or dead, business
establishments, events, or locales is entirely coincidental.

eBook ISBN-13: 978-1-7750832-3-8
Paperback ISBN-13: 978-1-7750832-2-1
Cover artwork and design by Konn Lavery.
Interior Illustrations by Yugen.
Photo credit: Nastassja Brinker.
Printed in the United States of America.
First Edition 2019.

Preface

You know, it's really funny how life takes twists and turns that you don't expect. When I came up with the idea for the Rutherford Manor Universe after a successful seasonal run of our Haunted House, my initial thoughts were really quite simple; do up a few comics, art, some new trading cards, and start to slowly build a brand with the stories and characters. I remember thinking that pop-culture is ready and waiting for a family of the horrific. Originally, the idea was to give Rutherford Manor a good solid five years and see what happens. I remember thinking, "Wouldn't it be cool to see someone cosplaying my characters at a comic or horror convention?" Little did I know those first thoughts would be the beginning of a wild ride toward that reality.

The production journey of Rutherford Manor is one of ups, downs, triumphs, and challenges. I look back at specific events and think, "This awesome outcome wouldn't have happened if that setback didn't occur." Isn't that so true in life? This journey has taught me when to blaze a new trail and when to go with the flow. I just never know what event or meeting will manifest something wonderful and new, as is true with the creation of this new book, The White Hand.

When I met Konn Lavery for the first time it was at the 2018 Calgary Horror Con. I was having a nice chat with horror legend George P. Wilbur while taking photos of him with the characters of Spalding, Nox, and Lilith. My wife, Karla, came to me and said I had to meet this young author on the other side of the hall. She brought me to his booth, introduced us, and showed me the books he was promoting. I immediately noticed a couple things about Konn - he is very dedicated to his writing and has an excellent presentation of his material, and, he is a man of good character, genuine, friendly, humble, and attentive. He certainly made a memorable first impression. We exchanged contact information and agreed to connect in Edmonton. A couple weeks later, Karla arranged a meeting with Konn to discuss the possibilities of collaborating on a new book for Rutherford Manor. It was then that this book you are about to enjoy took its initial steps from concept to reality. In other words, a chance meeting at a horror convention has now resulted in a new and amazing novel for the Rutherford Manor Universe. How cool is that?

This is only one of many stories of how Rutherford Manor has grown and attracted numerous talented people that see and understand my vision of this macabre world. Over the past few years I've been truly blessed to work with outstanding writers, artists, photographers, models, editors, haunters, game creators, actors, producers, directors, musicians, and other creative people in all areas of the brand. I've met incredible people through chance, introduction, social media, and conventions. I wouldn't change any of it! You all have my sincerest respect and thanks for everything you have done for me and the world of Rutherford Manor.

Working with Konn on this book has been so much fun and tremendously easy for me. His creative mind has taken many of the ideas and concepts that were mulling around in my head and brought them to life through my beloved characters in astounding ways. He has delved into the personality of the characters in a thrilling world of intrigue, mystery, emotion, and horror. Even as the creator of Rutherford Manor I found myself being pulled into the world deeper, enjoying every moment of the book, and anticipating what will happen next. To me, this is testament to the extraordinary writer that Konn is, and I can't wait to start working on the next one with him!

Now, in this book, the macabre story of the infamous inhabitants at Rutherford Manor begins. Your view on what the word 'family' really means, may be changed forever!

Preston Ewasiuk

Creator/Producer - Rutherford Manor

THANK YOU

A huge thank you to everyone that has been a part of the writing journey. I began perusing writing professionally in 2011. Writing has introduced me to many new people, cities, and events. It has pushed me to new frontiers. Each novel marks a milestone in the journey of storytelling. I believe that fiction is the best way to mask truths, educate, and inspire people. This is why I write. So, read into this book as much or as little as you'd like.

I'd like to give special acknowledgement to the people that helped bring this novel to life: Preston Ewasiuk, Neil Chase, Yugen, Ryley Shandro, Jordan Lesko, Lindsey Molyneaux, Karla Augert and everyone involved with the Rutherford Manor universe. The support and collaboration have been astronomical. Thank you for having me be a part of Rutherford Manor! Taking on such well-developed characters has been a humbling and exciting process.

Also, thank you to my long-time supporting friends and family: Brenda Lavery, Kyle Lavery, Terry Lavery, Kirra Lavery, Nastassja Brinker, Nick McQuade, Reg Black and Suzie Hess. The list can go on and I am grateful for each and every one of you. Unfortunately, the list would make a book of its own.

Lastly, but not least, I'd like to thank you, the reader. Your willingness to read this book is support on its own. You reading the novel is encouragement for me to continue my passion of storytelling. Now, enter Rutherford Manor and join the Fleshers and Savidges as they embark on a dramatic tale of survival!

Synopsis

Based on the award-winning Haunted House and forthcoming television series, The White Hand brings you into a historical thriller combining mobsters, forbidden love, old souls, murder, and betrayal.

Rutherford Manor — a safe haven for some. For others, a home that holds many sinister secrets. Run by the Fleshers and the Savidges, these two families have survived for generations leading up to the present day of 1890. Headmaster Alastor Flesher and his business partner, Spalding Savidge, find themselves in desperate times to provide for their families.

Their needs wrap them into a deal with the Irish mob — The White Hand. The two men willingly work with the gang as resurrectionists, obtaining bodies for anatomists. Alastor and Spalding develop a unique process, gaining access to the most well-preserved bodies. Their product becomes desirable throughout the black market in Illinois.

Despite the handsome pay, Spalding is left in disarray. Alastor's desperation for income runs deeper than he ever knew. His moral compass is shattered due to their snatching methods. Spalding plays with fire, developing something known as love for Irene, the daughter of The White Hand's boss. With a dash of foul play and new allies, Spalding becomes the glue that holds Rutherford Manor together, and he is coming unbound.

Join the Fleshers and the Savidges as they plummet into an era-altering series of events that will change Rutherford Manor forever.

TABLE OF CONTENTS

Preface

Thank You

ACT I: Denial

ACT I

DENIAL

CHAPTER 1

BEST ON THE MARKET

Meat is a funny thing. It is what consistently makes up people and living creatures. At the same time, it is also something we consume. It isn't hard to make the distinction between the flesh that you eat and the kind that you don't. Eatable meat is often defined by social and religious constructs. One side of the world says it is okay to eat a type of meat while another part says no. Before the flesh is considered eatable, an animal must be butchered, or die of natural causes. *Then* it is merely meat with no distinction of what it was when living. This applies to people too. We look oddly similar to animals when we've been mutilated.

This was messy, thought the man. The mutilated body he stood over was near death, gargling the blood that oozed from his mouth with each weakening breath. The man's boot pressed lightly against the trousers of the soon-to-be-deceased. He thought about moving but saw little point. It would take a lot more than pasty skin, open organs and a purple ribcage to induce nausea. Death did not bother him.

Truthfully, once you have been around enough flesh and death, you find the lines of horror and acceptance really begin to blur. Your notion of what is taboo and what is not dwindles. You find yourself on the outskirts of what it means to be human. The constant grimness leaves you balancing on the edge of your moral compass, not knowing if you will fall into darkness. In a way, you are in a fight for your own life—just like the butchered animals, and just like the mutilated man.

"Well, this should work nicely," said a second man, who gripped a crooked wooden cane, complete with a leather-bound chicken foot for the base. He stared down at the man on the floor whose breath continually softened.

"The open wound concerns me, Spalding," the first man said, looking down to his comrade's youthful face, half concealed in the shadow from his top hat.

"Think they will notice?" Spalding asked.

"Wouldn't you?" the first man returned.

Spalding extended his hand and shrugged. "I mean, this kind of thing I've gotten used to from you and my father. To a common lad? They might not know the difference at all. People get hurt all the time."

"Sounds like you've answered your question."

"Yes, I suppose? Maybe if I knew a thing or two about who we were delivering the body to, I could understand your concerns," Spalding said.

"The client is . . . not typical either," the first man replied while leaning down to grab the dead man's boots. "Come, let's get him wrapped up. Put that cane down. Why did you even bring that thing, anyway?"

"Out of respect," Spalding said while gently leaning the cane against a pillar, causing the black feathers from the top of the stick to dangle above a blackened skull tied to the rod.

"Respect for whom? I don't feel offended."

"My friend," Spalding said, looking at the skull.

"Ah, yes, Pierre Orléans. Didn't you kill him?"

"Aye, that was a bit of a hiccup. That was my first kill too." Spalding sighed, leaning down to take the body by the armpits. The two of them lifted the body up, manhandling him over to a large linen cloth laid on the dirt. They set him on the edge of the fabric, each grabbing a corner of the linen and wrapping it over the body. They then rolled the fabric and the body on the ground, wrapping it up to form a burrito. The muffled groans of the man were audible underneath the linen for a few moments, and then there was silence.

The first man stood up and looked around, examining the barn they stood in. The scene showed no evidence of the brawl they'd just had. No blood. No broken items. No one would know the difference.

A part of him wondered if anyone heard their fight with the farmer, but then again, this far out in the countryside, it was unlikely that anyone was nearby. The wife and kids had gone into town. The two of them were sure the farmer was alone.

"Alastor!" Spalding called out. "Give me a hand." He waved towards the large two-door barn entrance.

Both men marched to the door, pushing it open and exiting in the direction of the setting sun. They had parked their black carriage just outside of the barn. The ambush plan had been simple: They'd approached the man pretending they were lost and then beat him until he could no longer move.

Spalding walked up to the carriage, opening the back door, and hurried back to the barn.

"Let's get this body out of here," Alastor said while leaning down to the dead man's feet.

"Agreed," Spalding said as he took the head.

The two men lifted the linen-wrapped body and hurried over to the carriage. The corpse was a bit heavy for Alastor, and he panted with the effort. Perhaps if he were ten years younger, this wouldn't be a problem. Sometimes age had a funny way of being put on the backburner when you're in desperate times.

The body scraped the base of the carriage, and the two men dropped it with a thud.

"Good show," Spalding said with a smile.

"Yes, not bad for the first," Alastor said. He closed the door and snapped the lock shut, patting his peacoat's pocket to double-check if he had the key for it. Yes, he did.

"Okay," Alastor said. "We need to leave now if we want to make it to the meeting point in time."

"Right," Spalding said.

Alastor strolled around to the front of the carriage, waiting for Spalding to retrieve his cane. That weird killing-ritual item of his. Spalding returned, tucked the rod away, hopped onto the seat, and engaged their horse with a "Hiya!" The brown beast let out a snort as it began to trot along the path, kicking up dirt with each stomp of its hooves.

"When are you going to tell me more about this Bran Connolly character, our new client?" Spalding asked. "We're supposed to be partners."

"You're right," Alastor said. "Apologies for my secrecy."

"You've always been private, but never kept secrets like that. Our families are full of secrets, even before America, but there are no secrets between the Fleshers and the Savidges."

"I know. This one I wanted to be sure was a safe bet. It was for the protection of everyone."

Spalding reached into his pocket and pulled out a cigarette, putting one end in his mouth. He also grabbed a box and match. With one hand, he flicked the match and lit his smoke, saying, "Elaborate."

"They're the White Hand," Alastor said.

"White Hand? The Irish mob?" Spalding said while exhaling a lungful of smoke.

"That's correct. The White Hand are big players, rivalling the Italian Black Hand. They have a big influence in New York, but they are looking to expand in Illinois."

"Is that why you kept this deal secret until now?"

"I didn't want them to know who I was or anyone else to know what I was dealing with until I knew this was a solid deal."

"Gangs," Spalding said. "That's a first for us."

"They're businessmen and so are we," Alastor said. "They want our product, and we will sell it to them."

"I wish you hadn't kept me in the dark about this."

"It won't happen again. Please accept my apologies."

Spalding stared at him for a moment before nodding.

"You've got plenty to think about, anyway," Alastor said. "Where is Mrs. Savidge?"

Spalding let out a chuckle. "In the grave, if I reckon?"

"I mean your lack of a wife, not your mother." *Wise ass.*

Spalding shifted in his seat. "It'll happen, don't worry about it. We have so much to take care of already, like taking this dead bloke to the White Hand."

Alastor smirked. "You're just like your father. Charming to your advantage."

Alastor and Spalding's father had been partners before he passed away. Now, Alastor and Spalding found themselves as the head of their respective households, ensuring that the future generation would survive, and that starvation was not on the agenda.

The two rode in silence with the smell of tobacco filling the air until their carriage reached a hill. The horse trotted along, reaching the top where they now had a clear view of distant lights inside tall brick buildings overlooking a large expanse of water. Chicago.

"Whoa!" Spalding called out to the horse, bringing the animal to a stop. Tall grass surrounded the area; a light breeze moved the stems side to side. Blackness engulfed them. Only the lantern hanging from the carriage provided light. No one else was present.

"This is it," Alastor said while hopping off the carriage. He patted his back lightly to feel his sheathed dagger underneath his coat, confirming it was there just to relax his nerves. He wanted to be prepared in case their meeting went south.

Spalding got out of the carriage, unhooking the lantern, and walked over beside Alastor. "We're a bit early?" Spalding asked.

"Possibly. We'll wait," Alastor said.

The sound of galloping hooves picked up from the road leading to Chicago.

Alastor and Spalding stiffened their stance. Spalding kept his hands on his belt buckle, and Alastor had his hands cupped in front of him.

Three horses bobbed up and down with men on their backs, reaching the carriage. They skidded to a stop, allowing their riders to dismount. Sharp shadows cast over their forms from the lantern light. The three men, dressed cleanly in blazers and wide-brimmed hats, casually strolled towards the pair who waited.

Alastor scanned the three. He couldn't identify the two to his left but recognized the slim man to the right by his goatee.

"That's Bran, to our right," Alastor mumbled.

"The other two?" Spalding asked.

"Never seen 'em."

"Mr. Flesher," came the booming voice of Bran. He stopped about four meters from Alastor and Spalding. The other two men stood still, their hands extended out slightly as if they were ready to draw weapons.

"Bran," Alastor said while extending his hand, gesturing to the carriage. "We have what you requested."

Bran nodded. "Show us, then."

Alastor looked over at Spalding, and the two walked around to the back of the carriage. The three White Hand members followed as the fluttering of feathers came from the night sky. A grey owl landed on top of the carriage, its claws digging into the wood.

"Beat it!" Spalding waved his hands up at the animal a couple of times.

The owl flapped its wings and soared away through the air.

"Thank you," Alastor said while reaching for the key in his pocket. He took it out and unlocked the back door of the carriage, pulling it open.

The body in the back of the carriage was still wrapped up in the linen cloth.

Alastor stepped to the side, allowing the three men to see the wrapped-up body as Spalding raised the lantern for a clearer view of the blood-stained bundle.

Bran looked over at his two comrades. "Niles, Blyton."

The two White Hand members marched up to the carriage and pulled on the fabric, tugging it away and revealing the man's face.

One of the White Hand members placed his right hand on the man's lifeless cheek, tapping the body with a long finger wearing a black ring with three spikes. "Christ, it's still warm," he said, pulling back and brushing the dark hair from his face.

Bran let out a deep laugh. "Brilliant!"

Alastor smiled. "See? I told you we would provide the best on the market."

Bran walked to the carriage and placed his hand on the body. "Here I thought you would be nothing but jiggery-pokery."

"We may not be from around here, but we are no cons."

Bran stroked his goatee, saying, "I've never seen a resurrectionist bring one so fresh. Anatomists dream of this."

Spalding looked up at Alastor. He winked back, saying to

the group, "With this partnership, we'll change the market." Alastor knew from Spalding's expression it was one of those mixed looks his partner had given him in the past. A part of Spalding was obviously pleased with how the meeting was going, but he was also annoyed that he knew little of what their relationship with the White Hand was going to be. Alastor felt guilty for not sharing the news with Spalding sooner, but he couldn't. It wasn't worth the risk of endangering their family with the Irish mob until they had more information.

Bran waved his hand at the body, instructing his two goons to wrap up the corpse. He turned to face Alastor, his green eyes moving back and forth, analyzing him. "If I didn't know better, I would say you killed this man yourself."

Pretty good guess, Alastor thought. "Let's just say we have some experience in the business of the dead."

"Good enough for me." Bran extended his hand.

Alastor shook it firmly as the two men smiled at each other. He couldn't help but feel a wave of relief that the White Hand was pleased with what they'd provided. Their new business could be a source of good income.

Bran let go of Alastor's hand and followed his goons back to the three horses.

Alastor rubbed his chin, eyeing the animals. "You three going to be alright carrying it?"

"We got rope," Bran said as he stopped in front of one of the horses. He opened the saddle pouch and pulled out a tied-up linen bag.

Alastor looked over at Spalding, who was as wide-eyed as he was. That bag surely contained their payment.

Bran took a few steps towards them and then chucked the bag at them.

Spalding caught it and quickly unlaced the pouch to take a peek inside. Alastor leaned over to see a bag full of green paper—their earnings.

Rewarded as promised, echoed a wispy voice in Alastor's mind. Words of desire. He wasn't even sure if they were his own. He had been lost for so long trying to make coin; now, he had a large bag full of more than he could imagine.

"It's all there," Bran said while stroking his goatee. "Bring me another one of this quality next week, and I can see our business going spanking well."

CHAPTER 2

WELCOME HOME

Outcasts: a term that is used to describe those that are not part of the majority. Over the years the label had been used to describe the Fleshers and the Savidges time and time again. For the two families, being labelled as outcasts had created an odd sense of attraction towards the consistency of a commoner's life. Why were the families of Rutherford Manor so different?

A silver fork stabbed into a breakfast sausage. The link was still slightly red—tough meat to cook, or perhaps it was too scorched. A knife accompanied the fork to hack through the cooked flesh.

"With that kind of payment, we aren't going to have to keep eating this garbage," Alastor said.

The older man's deep voice caught Spalding's attention, and he looked up from his half-cut sausage. Alastor sat at the opposite end of the long dinner table. They were the only two at the table, with utensils, cups of coffee, and placemats.

"Aye, that is true," Spalding said. "No disrespect to the deceased, but I really am looking forward to a less game-tasting food."

"We'll have to go into town and get some items for dinner and celebrate the first White Hand deal," Alastor said.

"Yeah, we should. Will we have time for all of this?" Spalding asked.

"What do you mean?" Alastor asked.

Spalding waved his hands at the empty dining hall. "The manor is a bit empty as of late, ain't it?"

"Very true, Spalding." Alastor's tone softened. "Since Matilda passed, things haven't been the same for a while now. We need to bring new life to Rutherford Manor."

"What about Walter?" Spalding asked. He knew the question was a sensitive topic, but he had to be straight-up with his business partner. Spalding hoped that Alastor wouldn't think it was a passive-aggressive jab towards Alastor's recent secrecy. Spalding knew why the man had done it. He simply had to ask about Walter. Plus, transparency was crucial to Spalding.

"Walter?" Alastor said.

"Yeah, I figured your son might come back now that he has grown up in the world a bit. Realized that he just ain't like the rest." *Bold kid for trying,* Spalding thought.

"Walter is not coming back," Alastor said sternly. "He made it very clear he wants nothing to do with the family. He thinks he's better than us."

Spalding shrugged, saying, "I have to say it is daring to try and step out of generations of history."

"Anyway, in brighter news. . . ," Alastor said, changing the subject.

Still a sore topic, Spalding thought. At least Alastor was honest. Maybe the White Hand was a one-off.

". . . Vivian did get the letter that Nox is returning today," Alastor said. "I had sent one to him, after the accident."

"Right," Spalding said. "That poor boy. His arrival will help fill up the manor again."

"I have been informed that he has a lady of his own. A botanist."

"Interesting choice of study," Spalding said.

"Yes, she could potentially be an effective addition to the household. Not to mention a suitable candidate for carrying on the Flesher family name."

"Excellent, I am pleased to hear." *Here it comes,* Spalding thought.

"What about the Savidge name, Spalding?" Alastor asked.

"It'll happen in due time."

"You always say that. We're a decade away from the twentieth century. You need to start thinking about your future and stop wooing women's panties off any damn time you feel like it. You're a charmer, Spalding, I mean that in the brightest light, but you really use it in the wrong context. . . ."

As he always says, Spalding thought while having a sip of his coffee, tuning out his partner's words. Alastor still had his best interest in mind; Spalding couldn't hate him for that. But why couldn't he just leave this one topic alone? Women were beautiful, sophisticated, and plenty of fun. They also tired him easily.

". . . Anyway, I just want to urge you to think about settling down a bit," Alastor finished. Spalding had dozed off for a half a moment, missing Alastor's whole lecture. Probably for the better.

"Thank you, good sir," Spalding said while raising his cup at Alastor in a playful manner, clearly throwing his concerns to the side.

"Whatever happened to. . . ?" Alastor continued.

Drop it, Spalding thought. Now he was getting irritable.

"Janet? Jane? What was her name?"

"Jones, her name was Jones," Spalding said. "Besides, she was a dotty windbag. That wasn't going anywhere."

"You only saw her for a week."

"I know when I first see them. Jones was fun; that's all I was looking for."

Alastor shook his head and continued to eat his meal.

Finally. "So," Spalding said. "This body-snatching business of ours. . . ."

"Yes?"

"How did you end up contacting the White Hand?"

Alastor leaned back in his chair. "The right time and the right place, I suppose. With the White Hand expanding to Chicago, they need new forms of trade."

"Yeah, but body-snatching?"

"Weird one, isn't it? Lucky for us, anatomists in England aren't the only people curious about how we work. American doctors wish to explore our anatomy and bodies aren't readily available. At least we don't have to dig up graves."

"Aye, we got one up with our methods."

"That we do. We also avoid any chance of family members rioting for us digging up deceased loved ones."

"Well, I can imagine they'd try far worse if we were caught in the act of murdering their family."

"True," Alastor said.

"And you met Bran how?"

"In town."

"Without me?"

"I know, I know. I figured I could scope out more opportunities if I searched on my own time."

"Right."

"I heard about the White Hand from their street posters. After asking around, I found out that they're the Irish mob. They're big players."

"Oh yes, I know."

"Exactly. That is why I was cautious. I learned which bars they fancied and approached Bran about doing jobs. I had no idea it would lead to this."

"Body-snatching is risky. What if there were witnesses with that last snatch we did?"

"You were there too! The man was all on his own. As long as we are continually careful, we have nothing to worry about."

"One time we might slip up, and then we're in trouble. Like you say, Alastor, I'm just making sure that the families are protected."

"I appreciate your concern, Spalding, but this line of income is something we can't afford to lose."

"You trust the White Hand?" Spalding asked. "I don't."

"They're goons disguised as businessmen. We are real

29

businessmen. Bran and the White Hand are simply the middlemen carrying out the work for hungry anatomists."

"The *goon* part is what concerns me. This is the closest we've let outsiders become aware of how we can handle people. Ever."

"The White Hand doesn't know what our skills fully entail. We can outwit them."

Spalding wiped his face. *What are we doing with gangs? They're trouble,* he thought. He wanted to really drill in to Alastor what he really thought about the White Hand. But to what end? Survival was always Rutherford Manor's biggest struggle, it seemed. Spalding couldn't grasp why they couldn't simply open a butcher shop or start a farm. That would be less complex, wouldn't it?

A question that had gone unanswered for generations. Spalding's father couldn't explain it to him and nor could Alastor. They lived in the shadows and worked there; it was as simple as that. Body-snatching was now the name of the game. Alastor was convinced it was the right direction, and once the man made his mind up, there was no convincing him otherwise. Spalding was in for the ride with his business partner. Time to saddle up. Yippee ki-yay.

"Alright," Spalding said, finishing the last bite of his breakfast. "With that in mind, what is our next move?"

"The next snatch?" Alastor asked.

"Yeah, now that we are professional resurrectionists."

"Well, as Bran said, we meet at the same place and time next week. So, we should start scouting for a target."

"Preferably one without a family?" Spalding asked.

"If we can avoid it," Alastor said.

"We can't keep snagging farmers."

"It's discreet, though."

"Yeah, but they also talk a lot more," Spalding said. "If a bunch of farmers go missing, they're going to get on the defensive. They will get the law involved."

"Good point. what do you propose?"

"We hit Chicago."

"Really? What about all the witnesses? The distance?"

Spalding reached into his pants pocket to pull out a cigarette and match. He brought the butt to his lips and lit the match, puffing out a couple clouds of smoke. "There are more people and we're strangers there," he said. "Sometimes the best method is to hide in plain sight."

Creaking footsteps came from the second floor of the house. The sound grew louder as a young lady hurried down the stairs and into the dining room. She held her long white-and-red dress up to avoid dragging the material on the ground. A dirty doll was tucked between her forearm and hip.

Spalding took the smoke out of his mouth—he made it a rule to always be respectful in the presence of a lady. He glanced at the doll tucked under her arm and grimaced slightly. It always made him a little uncomfortable; she should have dropped that thing a good decade ago.

"Vivian, my dear, why are you in such a rush?" Alastor asked.

The girl's eyes were wide open. Her smile spread from cheek to cheek.

She is quite pretty—if you manage to remove the nutty look from her face. Maybe ditch the doll too, Spalding thought.

"Father!" Vivian exclaimed while pointing to the front door.

"Wonderful news."

"Yes?" Alastor asked again.

"Nox has made his arrival!" Vivian said. "Tammy and I saw his chariot approaching the manor."

Tammy the doll, Spalding thought. *That's why she's still single.*

Alastor stood up from his seat. "Wonderful indeed! I did not expect him to arrive so soon."

Vivian giggled and held up her doll. "Tammy didn't either."

"Of course," Alastor said. "Well, shall we greet the arrival of the future headmaster?"

Vivian let out a cheer and hurried out of the dining room towards the front door.

Spalding put the cigarette back in his mouth and let out a puff. "Nox? Head of the household?" He didn't want to judge his partner so harshly, but Spalding knew the kid, and he was no leader.

Alastor raised his arms. "What else do I have to work with?"

Spalding stood up. "True to that." The thought of working alongside Nox was not the ideal future for Spalding. The cold truth was that Alastor was older than Spalding. Eventually, he would be working with Nox, the bookworm Flesher. As far as Spalding knew, the kid had never thrown a punch in his life, let alone held an axe. Desperate times called for desperate measures, Spalding reflected. There was a pattern in Alastor's recent decision-making.

The two men exited the dining room. Spalding snagged his top hat as they left the foyer and emerged onto the veranda, awaiting the arrival of the youngest Flesher.

"Vivian," Spalding said while holding his smoke.

"Yes, Uncle Spalding?" Vivian asked with a toothy smile.

"May I?" he asked, waving his cigarette.

"Of course!"

Spalding nodded and continued to puff away.

The three stood in silence, staring out at the summer scenery of tall, green grass, lush trees, and a clear blue sky. Soon a chariot came into view in the distance. The horse pulling the carriage trotted along until it reached the front of Rutherford Manor.

A young boy sitting on the front of the carriage brought the animal to a stop and hopped off his perch. He was accompanied by a shorter blonde girl.

That's the last of the Flesher family tree, Spalding thought as he finished the remainder of his cigarette. Nox, the small, thin boy who dressed far too neatly to get his hands dirty. Well, except for the odd time that Nox had come along to help Spalding deal with Alastor's deeds. The kid was actually pretty quick when given the chance. However, he seemed different from the last time Spalding had laid eyes on him. He was sheepish in his walk, and kept his head low. The girl who walked with him appeared to take the lead in their steps. This was not the same Nox.

The accident, Spalding thought. He knew damn well what had happened to the boy back in university. Everyone did.

Alastor took one step down the staircase as the two newcomers approached the house. Nox looked up at his father, exposing the scar-covered half of his face. The skin had melted and fused in unnatural ways, making it difficult to see his one eye. Hairless and scabbed.

Alastor extended his arms, saying, "Nox, my dear son. It's

good to have you back."

"Th-th-thank you, Father," the boy slurred. His lips trembled slightly as he stuttered. The accident clearly had done more than just mangle his face.

Alastor turned to look at the girl and said, "Nox has written wonderful things regarding you. I trust he has said the same about us. You can consider Rutherford Manor your home."

"Thank you, Mr. Flesher," the girl said while curtsying.

"Please, call me Alastor," he replied.

Vivian let out a squeal and waved at the two newcomers. "Brother!" she said.

"Sister." Nox took a bow.

"Nox," Spalding said. "Pleasure to see you again."

"Th-th-thank you, Spalding. It-s-s good to be back," Nox slurred.

Spalding tilted his hat at the girl. "And what is your name?"

"Lilith," the girl said while extending her hand to him.

Spalding bowed and shook it politely.

Lilith retrieved her hand, saying, "And you must be Mr. Savidge. Nox has told me much about you and Rutherford Manor."

"We have quite the reputation, as I am sure you now know," Spalding said.

Alastor took a couple steps down. He said, "You two must be exhausted. Let's get your things inside."

The five walked down to the carriage and grabbed the luggage. Between them, it was easy to take all of Nox and Lilith's belongings and carry them into Rutherford Manor. Spalding, with the help of Lilith, held onto a steamer trunk. It was quite heavy and although Spalding thought he could take it himself, Lilith insisted on helping.

"I'll show Nox to his room," Alastor said. "Spalding, would you mind showing Lilith where she can stay? Let's use the second spare room."

"Of course," Spalding said while taking the lead to the second floor, holding the steamer trunk with his hands behind his back. Lilith took the back and the two of them hauled the trunk up to the second floor. Spalding wondered what was even in the trunk to make it so heavy. At the same time, it didn't matter; he just wanted to get the kids to their respective rooms so he could carry on with his day.

"I'm quite honoured to be here," Lilith said over the sound of the creaking wooden floor.

"I heard Nox is quite fond of you," Spalding replied.

"Yes, well," she panted, "he is a gentle soul. Troubled now after the explosion."

"And you were kind enough to keep Nox company in his time of sorrow. That shows a strong character."

"Thank you, Mr. Savidge."

Spalding led the girl to an empty, fully furnished room and dropped the trunk on the ground. "This will be your room for now. This spot good for the trunk?" he asked.

"Good for now," Lilith said. "Might move it to storage later."

Spalding turned to face the girl. Seeing her close up, he took notice of the dark rings under her eyes. "You must be tired. It might be best for you to get some rest."

"I could say the same about you, Mr. Savidge."

"Me? Tired?" Spalding smirked. "I just need to let out some

steam. Rutherford Manor has been a busy place despite the vacancy."

Spalding wished the girl farewell and exited the room. For an early day, there was a lot to digest—and not just the food, either. Rutherford Manor was shifting into a new era with Nox's arrival and the White Hand. The Flesher family's future looked bright. The Savidges, however, were as shrouded in uncertainty as always. Spalding didn't mind, though. Nothing a good dance wouldn't fix.

CHAPTER 3

FRIENDLY DANCE

Colliding skin. High force. Sweat. Shouting. Dim lighting cast over the fast-moving bodies that circled around one another. This was a brawl, where the excitement happened. A place like this was where men went to de-stress by throwing fists into each other's faces. It worked well. You'd be surprised how much you can decompress by throwing a few shots at another fellow. 'Satisfying' was the simplest way to put it.

"Show 'em who's boss, ya bloke!" came a shout from the crowd. It was impossible to tell where the voice originated from. There were so many men and women, drinking and smoking, and you could hardly see their faces in the smoky haze that filled the stone basement.

Knuckles grazed past dry lips, pressing into the jaw only for a split second before slipping away.

Close, Spalding thought while shifting his stance to avoid another swing from a mustached fellow. Both he and his opponent were covered in sweat, a bit of blood, and dirt. Spalding kept his head ducked low, shielded by his forearms, watching as the man in front of him panted heavily.

He's out of shape, Spalding thought. His last thought before zoning in on his target.

Spalding dashed forward and launched a false fist at the man. The misdirection caused his opponent to step into Spalding's second throw, which hit him straight in the jaw.

The crowd roared as the man's arms flew into the air and he stumbled backwards. He was wide open. Spalding threw another fist directly into his chest and then lashed a swift kick to the shin, tripping him in the process.

More cheers and claps erupted as drinks were raised in the air, splattering liquor onto the already drenched ground.

Spalding wiped his lip, realizing that blood oozed from it. He stared at his opponent, who remained on the ground, groaning.

"Good show, Jacob," Spalding said while extending his hand to him.

The man on the floor rubbed his jaw and accepted Spalding's hand. "Thanks. I don't know where you get that kind of speed from," he said, spitting a mixture of blood and saliva onto the floor.

"Practice," Spalding said. *Beating people to death helps too,* he thought.

He patted Jacob on the back and retreated into the crowd, retrieving his shirt from the ground in the process. He needed a drink. It was his first fight for the evening, and he hadn't been able to get the idea of the new business direction with Alastor out of his mind. Why was this crawling through his skin so much? He had a moral compass, but that never seemed to be an issue before. Maybe he was getting soft as he got older.

Spalding gathered his pay for the fight from one of the organizers—a big bald guy who continually thirsted for bloody fights. The man's desire to watch extreme violence was worrisome. All Spalding did was fight for the sport. He didn't want to inflict pain. At least the organizer gave Spalding a way to rumble. The regular crowd put bets on Spalding's fights. It was never much, but it was enough to buy a drink or two.

After obtaining his pay, he took the coins and dropped some onto the bar with a clang. The noise caught the bartender's attention. He stepped forward and brought both hands onto the counter, saying, "What can I get for ye?"

"Pint," Spalding said.

The bartender snagged the coins with one hand, and a pint glass in another. Glass filled and returned. Spalding took a chug back, embracing the crisp ale with his blood-coated tongue. Spalding watched the two other rings of fighters, keeping his back against the bar. One of the rings was concealed by the crowd, while the second one was easier to see.

In it a thin man was battling against a much larger man with a long black ponytail. The scrawny guy didn't seem to stand much of a chance as the large man lunged a foot forward, then made a full swing of his fist. His attacks were impressively fast for his size.

"Didn't know we let Indians fight with civilized folk!" shouted a man at the bar. "Savages have an unfair advantage."

Spalding looked over at him, nostrils flaring. The racial slurs were unfortunately all too common; it was a part of life. One would have hoped that, a hundred years after the revolution, things might have been different. Unfortunately, that wasn't the case. In a different sense, Spalding understood what it was like to be an outcast. Outcasts, shunned for not fitting in with the majority.

"Can ye believe that?" the man at the bar said again. Droplets of either beer or spit drizzled down his long beard as he shouted, "I didn't come here to watch a redskin make a—"

Spalding cut the man's statement short. "I didn't come here to listen to you spew bigotry either."

The man's mouth remained open as he turned to look at Spalding with glazed-over liquor eyes. "Wudd'ya say to me?" he asked.

"Your tongue spits poorly educated statements and, quite

frankly, irritates me."

"Ye one of them Rutherford folk, aren't ye?"The man swayed as he walked closer to Spalding. The scent of sweat and piss drifted up from his body.

A mix of cheers and boos came from the crowd as the large man threw the fight-ending blow into the smaller man's face.The noise distracted the drunk from Spalding; he had an attractive opportunity. One fist to the bigot's face would shut him up for good. No. He resisted.This was a fight club; it wasn't a free-for-all brawl. As much as Spalding wanted to shove his fist down the man's throat, there wasn't a point unless he could get him into a ring.That was the fight club's rules. Another man leaned against the bar on the other side of Spalding, his mustached opponent. Jacob got his own drink and raised it to Spalding.

"Good fight," Jacob said.

"Aye," he said, turning to face him.

"Oi!" slurred the drunk behind him.

Spalding ignored him as the drunk muttered something inaudible under his breath. It was probably more idiotic statements.

Jacob took a sip of his beer. "There's a lot of new faces here, eh?"

Spalding nodded. He personally hadn't taken note of the increased crowd. His mind was too lost in his own issues and he didn't really focus on his immediate surroundings. Taking a look around, he saw Jacob was telling the truth. Spalding could maybe identify half of the crowd. Unfamiliar faces meant new women. There were always ladies at the fight club watching men beat each other up in the name of sportsmanship. It was probably a turn-on for them. Whatever the case, it was a nice perk.

"Well," Spalding said, "new faces here means things are moving up for the town of Rowley."

"Yeah, this is good news for all of us. We need more folk here," Jacob said.

The two watched as the ponytailed man lumbered over to the bar, standing beside Jacob. He had little sweat and no blood on him. His scrawny opponent really had no chance.

Spalding raised his glass at the man. "Good show!"

The man looked over at him with a worn face and flat eyebrows.

"The name is Spalding," Spalding said.

"Billy," the man said.

"Jacob," Jacob added.

Billy got his drink from the bartender and walked away.

"Not a very friendly guy, is he?" Jacob said.

"Can't blame him, considering the crowd," Spalding said.

Jacob took a big gulp of his drink, slamming it down onto the bar. "You're right there. I'm going to piss. Catch you later, chum." He patted Spalding on the back and walked away.

Spalding scanned the crowd, looking at the range of new faces, and the ladies. He was looking out for pretty women specifically. There were a few he didn't consider to be up to his standards and gazed over them. The narrow hourglass shape was a preference. It helped if they had a decent bust and a rear to admire. Perhaps one would accompany him under the sheets tonight. It was a much more enjoyable hunt than body-snatching. This was his issue, he knew. He saw it as no more than a game. How could he settle down, marry, and have children if he kept this mindset up all the time? It seemed impossible. What the hell did Alastor know, anyway?

Through the crowd Spalding's wandering eye caught sight, not of a woman, but a dark-haired man in a vest sitting at one of the tables alone. His hand—holding a beer—had a black three-spiked ring on it.

That's someone I didn't expect to see here, Spalding thought, recognizing the man as one of the White Hand goons that had accompanied Bran the day before.

Spalding grabbed his drink and wandered over to the table, sitting down next to the man. "What a surprise to see you here," he said.

The dark-haired man's eyes looked up at Spalding, brushing his long nose with his right hand, exposing the three-spiked black ring. He straightened his posture and raised a glass. The two men clinked their pints with a loud clang.

"I could say the same to you," the man said.

"Apologies, we never had a formal introduction," Spalding said.

"Niles," said the man.

"Spalding."

"Pleasure, Spalding."

"Likewise. So, are you looking to observe, bet, or partake tonight?"

Niles smirked. "I'm keeping my options open. Honestly, I haven't seen much of a challenge here. Seems unfair if I participated."

"You talk a big game." Spalding took a sip of his beer.

"We also use these types of places as recruitment."

"Really? Any keen interest?"

"Not tonight. Usually, I sniff out the clubs in Chicago but thought I'd test my luck elsewhere."

Spalding finished his drink, slamming it down on the table. "Well, could I interest you in a brawl with me? Friendly, no cash involved. At least to start with."

Niles let out a laugh.

Spalding stared at him, waiting for him to get the idea through his head that Spalding was not joking.

Niles's smile faded, and he leaned back in his chair, saying, "Ever do an Irish stand-down?"

Spalding shook his head. "No, can't say that I have nor know what that is."

"It's traditional bare-knuckle fighting where the aspect of maneuvering around the ring is removed."

"Interesting."

"It leaves only punching and taking punches. Interested?"

"I'm game," Spalding replied.

Niles extended the hand with the black ring, and Spalding shook it firmly. He smiled at him. "Let's do this."

Perhaps this will be a decent dance, Spalding thought. He could use a challenge, something to really keep his mind off of being a professional resurrectionist. Something to completely shift his focus.

The two men got up from their seats as a narrow gal in a white blouse and a vest arrived. Her hands were on her belt as her green eyes moved back and forth from Spalding and Niles. "Where the hell do you think you're going?" she asked, her red locks dangling over one eye.

Now that is a gal, Spalding thought as his eyes ran up her boots, legs, and breasts, peeling away her slim-fitting clothing with his imagination. He moved all the way up her sharp exposed clavicles and to the tiny freckles on her cheeks. What a gem. Not often did he see a lady dressed in such unconventional style, but a lady was a lady once you took the fashion away.

Niles nodded at Spalding, saying, "We're going to have a friendly dance."

The girl raised a naturally thin eyebrow. "We're here to recruit, not play around."

"Pardon me, my lady," Spalding said, taking a slight bow before extending his hand. "Spalding."

The girl looked at his gesture, keeping her hands on her belt. "Irene."

Spalding put his hand down. "Pleasure." *Hard to play with. I like that.*

Gunfire erupted. The bang reverberated against the stone walls of the basement, amplifying the sound. Several screams, and a second shot roared. People began moving in a hurry, blending throughout the room, making it impossible to tell where the sound had come from.

Who brings a gun to the fight club? Spalding thought.

"Christ!" Irene hissed, grabbing hold of her hat.

Niles leaned to Spalding's ear. "Looks like our game will be postponed."

Unfortunately, he was right. Audience members ran across the fight rings. Some unscheduled fistfights broke out in the crowd, and people hurried up the stairs to leave the basement.

One man even picked up a chair and swung it at an unexpecting passerby.

"Niles!" Irene shouted. "Let's hotfoot!"

Spalding shrugged. "Best get my things and leave this chaos."

"Likewise. Be well," Niles said before joining Irene as the two retreated to the staircase.

Can't people hold their liquor? Spalding thought, generalizing the random gunshot issue. It had ruined his opportunity for a potential brush and a good fight.

Spalding hurried over to the bar where he'd stashed his belongings with the bartender earlier. Thankfully, Spalding was a regular, and it was never an issue. Top hat and coat acquired. It was time to navigate through the mess and back to regular life. Well, as regular as his was.

CHAPTER 4

A SIMPLE VIVISECTION

Time: something that we all experience and have little understanding of. The clock ticks at a consistent pace, yet the dimension has a funny way of speeding up as one gets older. In childhood, a full day lasts a lifetime. As an adult, a week can feel like nothing. A week which consists of seven lifetimes for a child. Seven lifetimes can create a lot of memorable experiences, especially if they are not enjoyable ones. Hunger and poverty are not ideal memories for a child.

Poverty was never part of Alastor's game plan. He wanted to blame some boogeyman or demon for the families' problems, but he knew that was not the case. Times were tough in America. There wasn't a lot of work, and there weren't a lot of openings. Now he and Spalding had a chance to change it. Rutherford Manor finally had the opportunity to grow, thanks to Nox returning with his new lady companion. Alastor was hopeful for their future. As long as he and Spalding stayed on top of their duties, they could make a healthy living.

No more improvised meals, Alastor thought while puffing on a cigar.

At the cost of the agreement. A wispy voice ran through his mind. The haunting voice that reminded him of what he had done. It wasn't something to worry about now. At the moment, he could enjoy his cigar on the veranda of Rutherford Manor, knowing he could provide for his family.

One week had passed since Spalding and Alastor caught their first body for the White Hand. The cash from the body was good. It also wasn't enough to sustain them. The two were to meet with Bran today and provide a new corpse. First, they needed to have a body. The partners had discussed options throughout the week and ultimately decided that a random choice was their best way to remain undetected. There was such a thing as overengineering your strategy.

Enter Chicago. Blend in. Observe. Target. Stalk. Strike. Poison, Alastor thought. The plan was simple and, in theory, effective. Similar to their previous engagement but ideally with less violence and brute force. Unlike the first body-snatching, they had a secret weapon: Alastor's clever son, Nox.

Alastor finished his cigar while Lilith and Vivian walked up to the veranda carrying baskets of laundry.

"Vivian, Lilith," Alastor said with a bow.

"Mr. Flesher," Lilith said with a curtsey.

"How has everyone been treating you?" Alastor asked. "I see we haven't scared you away yet."

Lilith giggled and replied, "Of course not. Nox's words speak the truth of this home. Everyone has been very welcoming. Vivian has been a wonderful guide."

"Aw, thank you!" Vivian said with a wide grin.

"I am pleased to hear you are enjoying your stay. We take very few into the manor, and those that we do are family to us."

"Thank you," Lilith said. "As I am sure Nox has told you, I don't have one of my own in America." Her voice trembled.

"In letter form, yes, not in person. Your expression tells so much more," Alastor said. "Lilith, my dear, do you know how the solution is coming along?"

"Nox and I have been testing it throughout the week. He should have it for you in his study."

"Excellent, that is exactly what I was hoping to hear." Alastor got up from the chair and returned into the manor with the two girls. They split ways as he went around to the staircase leading to the second floor, then the third. The third set of stairs led to the top level of the manor where the attic was. The steps were narrower and creaked far more than the others.

Eventually, we can get that fixed. Just need to get more bodies, Alastor thought.

He pulled open the door and entered the top level of the manor. The dark room was only lit by a lantern and a small circular window in the center of the room. Off to the corner with the lamp was a boy hunched over a desk littered with metal contraptions, sealed jars with liquids, and an array of surgical tools.

Alastor had visited the study a few times before Nox returned and was familiar with most of the items. There were some new devices on the floor, though. It pleased Alastor to see his son

working away at his practice again, and so thoroughly in just one week. The sight of his son in the study brought back memories of when the house was full. Of when both of his sons were here, and his wife.

Matilda, my dear, Alastor thought, feeling his heart turn heavy. How he missed her. Her passing had come all too soon. Their sons needed a motherly figure in their lives. Unfortunately, that was never to be. Alastor never had any luck in marrying again. His heart was too heavy, his life too complex. What type of woman would want to be involved in this mess? Perhaps Spalding found himself in a similar situation, and that was why he has not married. Or maybe if he stopped vanishing after a night of passion, Alastor reflected, a lovely lady would stick around.

"Nox," Alastor said. His footsteps echoed as he lumbered over to his son.

Nox looked over at his father. He had a monocle strapped to his undamaged eye. "F-f-father," he murmured.

"Lilith tells me the solution is pretty much ready?" Alastor stopped in front of the desk, where a small pigeon was strapped to a metal plate. The organs spilled out of the animal as red liquid drizzled underneath the feathers. This was fresh. Nox had to have cut the creature open moments ago.

"Y-y-yes father. I used it on the bird here."

"It's still alive?" Alastor asked, leaning closer to the creature. Blood pumped out of the animal in a steady beat; the heart was moving. Small tubes were on each end of the animal's heart. One pumped blood out into an empty jar, and the other injected a translucent green liquid.

"See? It is un-un-aware of what is happening. Lilith put together the final ingredients in the mixture."

"It feels nothing?"

"Perfectly asleep after injection."

"Stunning." Alastor placed a hand on his son's shoulder. This was exactly what they needed for tonight. "How long does it take to have an effect?"

"Not long, a f-few seconds. They become disoriented and scared before their limbs seize."

"That is perfect. Will there be enough for the size of a man?"

"Of course; I have some prepared. We c-can also reproduce it easily with Lilith's plants. She is currently repotting her garden in the back la-a-awn."

"Good. I see your ability to dissect this animal has improved since you went to university as well."

Nox turned to look at the animal, slurring, "Y-y-yes. Animals of this size are fairly easy. Their whole body is right in front of you."

"What are you doing to this one, anyway?" Alastor asked.

"S-s-seeing if we can replace blood with another fluid. A better fluid than blood."

"What is better than our own blood?"

"A hybrid of the solution I made for you. I h-h-hope to have it dry quicker when exposed to air, working quicker to scab over a wound." He widened his arms, showing a large length between his palms. "I-I-I'd like to explore larger creatures. See if this solution can w-w-work on other forms."

Alastor stroked his chin. "Let's keep that in mind." *Maybe I can help get him some specimens,* Alastor thought. Just because

Nox was at home, away from the university, it didn't mean he couldn't continue to expand his mind.

"Nox, may I have the solution? Spalding and I will be leaving soon," Alastor said.

Nox put down his tools and leaned over to a stack of papers. The papers were rough sketches of dissected animals, organs, and bones. The boy was also a talented illustrator. He might not have raw strength, but he'd mastered skills Alastor couldn't even fathom doing.

Beneath the papers was a small black tin case. The boy took it and handed it to his father.

Alastor flicked it open. Inside, a syringe was fully loaded with a yellow-tinted liquid. "Beautiful. Full dose?"

"We believe so. It has yet to-to be tested on a human."

"We'll let you know how it turns out," Alastor said while closing the tin. "You managed to do all of this in one week? You are truly astonishing."

"Th-th-thank, you, Father. It just makes sense to me. Other things d-d-don't."

"What do you mean?" Alastor leaned down to be eye-level with his son.

Nox lifted his monocle and pointed at the bird. "This bird is beautiful. It can fly. Why can't humans fly?"

Alastor smirked. "Because God did not make us so. We have our minds and souls."

"I see. Humans only have souls?"

"Yes. God never gave them such a thing. We are blessed in many other ways."

"How are we b-b-blessed?"

"Well, we have the ability to critically think. We can see, touch, and feel."

"Th-then why did God punish me with this?" Nox pointed at his scarred face. "Why, F-f-father? Why did God take Mother too?"

Alastor sighed and looked to the ground. He couldn't come up with a good reason to explain the injustice to his son. Truthfully, it put his own faith in question. Then again, all of the hardships the family experienced would be enough to pull any man away from religion. But Alastor believed there was always hope.

"We just need to keep holding on. We are still a family, and God will bless us so." He rose from his kneeling position. "With your talent and our new business, we will get back up on our feet."

"I'd l-l-like to join in on the family business," Nox said.

"In due time. I greatly appreciate that you took my letter seriously and returned home to us."

"I kn-know. We discussed this last week," Nox said. To a newcomer, the boy's literalism and blunt way of speaking would come across as rude. That was not the case for Alastor. It was a delightful part of the boy's personality.

"We did indeed," Alastor said. "I want to revisit that, eventually, you will be taking control of the household. We'll get you familiar with the family business. Perhaps next summer once you have had time to settle in back here."

"Wha-what about Walter?" Nox asked.

Alastor pressed his lips together tightly, and he looked away for a moment. The name was always a sharp pain in the heart.

How could his eldest son walk out on him? On this family? Especially when they needed him most—when Matilda had passed.

"Well," Alastor said, clearing his throat, "Walter is unlikely to come back anytime soon. It is just us now."

"An-and Uncle Spalding?" Nox asked.

"Correct. You will learn to work closely with him." Alastor patted his son on the shoulder to reinforce his good work before he stepped away. "We'll be back in the evening."

"Good luck, Father," Nox said.

Alastor exited the study, returning to the main floor. He was grateful to have his family partially reunited. Having both of his sons gone and his wife passing had been difficult beyond what he could handle. At least one of the three was able, and willing, to return to the family home.

CHAPTER 5

THE PERFECT MATCH

Spalding and Alastor left Rutherford Manor by midday. Their travel from the homestead into Chicago would take a decent portion of the afternoon and then they could begin the hunt. A part of the task was exciting—payment—and a part of it was unsettling. If they stuck to their plan, they could find an unfortunate soul that wouldn't be missed. Basically, they were looking for a waste of life. That could justify their actions, couldn't it?

Most likely not. The disruption of the moral high ground aggravated Spalding. Why was he so torn about trying to justify his own survival? He'd seen the reward coin for their last snatch. Why wasn't that enough to keep him motivated?

Spalding lit a cigarette and looked to the scenery away from Alastor. His thoughts continuing to run through questions of right and wrong about the task at hand.

"You are quiet today," Alastor said.

Spalding took the cigarette out of his mouth. "Not much to discuss, is there?"

"I suppose not. You usually have more to comment about, that is all."

"It appears I don't have much to offer today."

Alastor pointed at Spalding's lip. "I see that hasn't healed very well."

"It is of little concern to me, really," Spalding said.

"Anything unusual go down at the fight club, got you silent?" Alastor asked.

"There was a gunshot. Not totally abnormal. Some sore loser can't handle defeat and ruins everyone else's fun." Spalding snapped his fingers, saying, "Oh, yes. I did run into Niles." *And a stunning lady,* Spalding thought. *The gal that left all so prematurely before I could woo her.*

"Niles . . . one of Bran's men?" Alastor asked.

"Yeah, he's the dark-haired one. He was there with a lady looking to recruit. He wasn't really interested in fighting."

"Interesting. I suppose the White Hand have to look somewhere to get men."

Their carriage came to the crossroad with a split path, one way leading to the town of Rowley and the other Chicago. Their route was crossed by a lone man on a horse. He had a gold badge pinned to his long coat, a vest and a bullet belt—indicators that he was a man of the law. Spalding knew him. Alastor knew him. Rowley's sheriff, Jenson Miller.

Alastor leaned closer to Spalding, whispering, "We're going into the city to see if we can gain new business deals."

"For what?" Spalding asked.

"Afternoon, gentlemen," the sheriff called out.

"Howdy," Spalding said, tipping his hat.

"Evening, sheriff," Alastor said while bringing the carriage to a stop.

"You two headed into Rowley?" the sheriff asked, halting his horse.

Alastor halted their carriage, parallel with Sheriff Jenson.

"Not today, I'm afraid. We are heading to Chicago."

"That's a bit of a ride, is it not?" Jenson asked. "What brings you out there?"

"We're going to see if we can round up some new business," Spalding said.

"I suppose you're right there. You know, there are some unfilled niches in Rowley. You folk could come into town and leave that old manor behind."

Alastor cleared his throat. "We are not leaving Rutherford Manor."

Sore spot, Spalding thought. He knew Alastor well, and any time someone belittled the value of the manor, it sent him into a rage. His father and his grandfather before him had contributed to the Fleshers and Savidges being in America, and Alastor didn't dare dishonour them by leaving.

"We'll think about it, sheriff," Spalding said. "Truthfully, funds are a little low I'm afraid. We need to do what we can for now. Who knows, perhaps our meetings can bring more people and industries to Rowley?"

The sheriff nodded. "Truth to that. See if you can razzle-dazzle those city-folk."

"Will do. Thanks, sheriff," Spalding said.

"Hiya!" Alastor commanded his horse, and the carriage picked up momentum.

"Wouldn't hurt to make more of a community effort," the sheriff called out. "You and your families might not be considered such outsiders!"

The carriage continued on, leaving the mounted sheriff in the distance.

"Bastard," Alastor muttered underneath his breath. "Always been sticking his nose in where it doesn't belong."

"Aye, that's his job, though, especially in a small town such as Rowley. We're not there all the time, and it makes them uncomfortable. Not to mention people wonder how we manage to stay alive being so secluded. We're not farmers."

"None of their concern." Alastor let out a sigh. "Well done covering that up, though. I don't think he suspected anything."

Spalding finished his smoke and flicked it away.

Their ride into the city was uneventful and long, much like the previous week, taking up the rest of the afternoon. It was one that Spalding didn't care for because they arrived back home in the early hours of the morning. For now, it was a necessary step to getting this dirty deed done.

Their carriage slowed as it reached the roads of Chicago leading to the city's core. The streets were littered with people carrying about their daily business. Hundreds of them moving in and out of buildings, talking to street merchants or riding on their own wagons. They even spotted a horseless buggy. The city made Rowley look minuscule in comparison.

All these people, Spalding thought. *One of them is going to die today.* It was a grim idea. Something Spalding had been through plenty of times before. That moral compass of his whispering in the back of his mind.

"I've never been much for the big city," Alastor said.

Spalding nodded, trying to shake off his inner whispers. "Not quite something I've grown accustomed to yet. I suppose we will need to learn to do so with this body-snatching business."

"That we will. Let's park the carriage and see if we can spot any suitable candidates," Alastor said. "Wasn't there an evening marketplace near 35th?"

"I believe so. It's worth a shot," Spalding said.

Alastor nodded. "Keep an eye out for a candidate who has a low profile and won't be missed."

"Shame we can't just pick some homeless folk," Spalding said.

"Too infested with disease. We want to give the White Hand quality bodies, not rotting ones."

The two navigated through the busy streets, following signs until they arrived at a market. They hopped down from the carriage, tied up the horse and locked the wagon wheels. In a town of this size, they couldn't leave their carriage unattended.

"Spalding!" Alastor called out.

"Aye?" Spalding replied as he finished setting the locks on the wheel.

"Get over here."

Spalding hurried around to the front of the carriage where Alastor leaned into the wagon. He got up onto the seat to see that his partner was pointing at his cane.

"You brought it?" Alastor whispered.

"Yeah, I couldn't leave Pierre behind. We're about to make another kill."

Alastor shook his head. "That is a goddamned skull on stick! What if someone goes through our stuff?"

"We'll lock it up. Don't worry. I'm no fool and not going to bring it in public. It's just a—"

"An honour thing. I know. You're a man of respect." Alastor sighed. "Just make sure it is good and locked up, okay?"

"Of course," Spalding said while Alastor got out of the carriage.

Sorry, Pierre, Spalding thought while eyeing the cane. That kill. His first kill. Maybe it was responsible for what led him down the left-hand path into this life. It is true what they say, he thought: Once you make your first kill, there is no going back.

Spalding finished locking up and hopped off the carriage. He stood up to come face to face with a simple black-ink-covered paper with a white hand in the center nailed to the wooden post.

"Look at that," Alastor said. "It appears Bran is making his presence known."

"What's the point to that?" Spalding asked.

"Awareness. The White Hand wants the people to know who is boss in Chicago." Alastor reached into his peacoat pocket and pulled out a pipe. "Have a match?"

"Aye," Spalding said, pulling out a match and a cigarette of his own. He lit both of their smokes and extinguished the flame.

The market stretched long down the street, with shop owners extending their storefronts with outdoor tables. Wagons were in the middle of the road, creating pop-up shops. The streets were compact, making it impossible for any vehicles to move through. This road was foot-only.

Men hauling goods, families shopping, people managing tables, everyone busy with their lives. They mostly wore beautiful bright clothing, a new fashion that Spalding wasn't familiar with. He didn't come into Chicago too often unless there was an agenda. The clothing was nothing like what they wore in Rowley. The men sported blazers, and the women were snugly fitted into shorter dresses.

No women, Spalding thought. That was not why they were here. Alastor and Spalding were on business.

So many walks of life in this city. How do we know who to pick? Spalding thought. He knew that Alastor didn't care at all—that much was clear from the last one they'd snatched. But Spalding wanted to be ethical in their choices. The sun was slowly beginning to set in the distance. The market would soon come to a close, meaning the two would have to make a decision before long.

A brunette girl carrying a basket full of bread approached Spalding and Alastor. She kept her head low and held the basket with both hands. She looked up at them with piercing blue eyes. *Stunning.*

"Would you care to buy some bread?" the girl asked in a silky voice. It was a sound Spalding was drawn to. Her words melted in his head and he could only focus on her puffy pink lips moving.

Alastor took his pipe out of his mouth and spoke up. "No, that's alright. Thank you, though."

"Are you sure?" the girl asked. "We're having a two-for-one sale today."

"No, my lady, please move along," Alastor said.

Spalding realized he still had his smoke in his mouth. How rude.

Alastor chuckled.

"What?" Spalding asked, taking a puff, watching as the bread-selling girl's hips swayed side to side as she walked away.

"She had you starstruck there, didn't she?" Alastor asked.

"Yeah, some ladies will do that to me. Dangerous, ain't it?" Spalding said.

Alastor shook his head. "Let's stay on topic, shall we? I'd say this market closes soon and that's when we follow our target."

A middle-aged man caught Spalding's attention. He used a cane and walked alone through the busy streets. People moved around him as he struggled with his bags. Spalding casually used his smoke to point at him. "What about that man with the cane? We could pretend to help carry his things to his home."

Alastor stared at the scene for several moments and then nodded at the general direction. "The family."

"What?" Spalding asked.

"The family by the bread stand. A husband, wife, and child."

"A whole family? We only need one." Spalding asked.

"True. But I want to see if we can step up our game from last week. What do you think Bran will do if we show up with two bodies? He'll cough up more."

Greedy was the one word that came to Spalding's thoughts. Why did they need to take on more than what they needed? "I think we should play conservatively here," Spalding said. "Maybe gamble with more bodies later. Let's stay true to our word. Besides, what if the White Hand says no to the extra body?"

"Well, Nox is looking for some bigger bodies to work with

for his studies."

Spalding exhaled heavily. He didn't like this. Not one bit. Alastor was pushing their luck. "What of the boy?" Spalding asked.

"Crossfire damage. It happens all the time."

That's a line, Spalding thought. He wasn't sure why it was a line. Hell, he didn't even have kids. Why was someone else's brat suddenly his concern?

"Spalding." Alastor took his pipe out of his mouth and stepped closer to his partner. His long graying hair blew in the subtle breeze. Alastor towered over him, as he did with everyone else. He was like a walking scarecrow.

"Spalding," he repeated. "Listen to me. The family is the better option."

"Elaborate," Spalding said.

"First, both the father and mother are younger than the target you picked out. They're also younger than the one we went for last week."

"So?"

"Anatomists dream of having young bodies to research. They're rare. Old gizzards are a dime a dozen."

"We didn't come here to kill families. What about yours?"

"I'm not about to have my family starve to death so some other ungrateful family can live on." Alastor pointed to the crowd. "Look at these people. We're not like them, and they will never know the depths that we've been through to survive. Believe me, when the White Hand sees what we can get, they will pay more."

Spalding could not disagree with Alastor. The little he did

know about the resurrectionist business was that scientists and doctors were hungry. There was a lack of knowledge of the human body. They were willing to pay dirtbags like Bran to do the work. The White Hand liked to keep their hands clean, so, shit rolled downhill, as they say. That left the desperate to do the dirty work. The desperate in this case being the Fleshers and Savidges.

"How long?" Spalding asked, staring at the family who was now paying for their goods. *Naïve.*

"How long for what?" Alastor asked.

"How long will we be working as resurrectionists?"

Alastor bit his lip, also watching the family. He thought about the question for several moments. It was clear to Spalding that his partner hadn't even considered their exit strategy. He was getting lustful for the potential money.

"Enough for us to get through the winter and open up a legitimate business," Alastor said.

"Like what?" Spalding said.

"Well, I was thinking something in Rowley. Any preference?"

Spalding finished his cigarette and flicked the end into the street. What could the Savidges and Fleshers do with a legitimate business? That was a question he hadn't thought seriously about. His father and Alastor were always running the shady types of work to raise coin. Moonshine, drugs, stolen artifacts, animal trading, you name it.

Perhaps Alastor was getting tired of the game too. The man was older than Spalding and had a son to think about. Maybe this would finally be it. Pierre would be able to retire also.

"We seem to gravitate to dealing with the dead," Spalding

said. "How about a butcher shop?"

Alastor chuckled and extended his hand. "Deal."

Spalding shook it firmly. The transparency was real, something that Spalding was grateful for. Alastor still had a mind of his own. He had secrets too. However, now that they had set some boundaries to their body-snatching agreement, Spalding felt more at ease. There would be an end to this darkness, and perhaps they could live like ordinary folk and not outcasts. Well, maybe they could just blend in with them.

CHAPTER 6

FRESH CATCH

Nighttime. The half of the day where light is little. When children are fearful for what lurks in the dark unknown. And rightfully so; evil people and monsters tend to hide in the shadows. Perhaps the unknown is what they are really terrified of. It is indeed a realistic fear in adulthood. The unknown. Uncertainty brews paranoia. Darkness is the canvas of nightmares.

"There they go," Alastor said while keeping himself pressed against the brick wall of a convenience store. He acted as if he were talking to Spalding, who faced him. The trick to stalking is to blend in, so no one batted an eye. Especially if you were two men on an empty street, only a block away from a lonesome family.

Spalding casually looked over to see the family had come to a stop. They were in a quiet neighbourhood without a lot of activity. Most homes had their lights off. No pedestrians. This

69

could potentially be an easy snatch.

The family unlocked their front door and opened it wide, entering and closing the door behind them. Their home was one of several dozen lining the street. The stalking session had taken them a good half-dozen blocks away from the marketplace where they'd left the carriage.

"Okay, we'll let them settle in so they unwind and put their kid to bed," Alastor said.

Spalding sighed. "Are you positive that this is the best course of action?"

"Spalding," Alastor started, "we've been through this. Not to mention that the White Hand have yet to receive a woman's corpse. They'll be thrilled." He reached into his pocket and pulled out a black tin. Popping it open, there was a syringe needle, fully loaded.

"What's that?" Spalding asked.

"Something my son and Lilith conjured up. I saw it injected in one of his animals. Quite impressive."

"What's it do?"

"Paralyzes them," Alastor said with a grin as he pulled out the syringe and tucked the tin back into his pocket.

Typical of a Flesher. Always a new trick up their sleeve, Spalding thought. The words in his mind upset him, considering the family had always been good to him and his kin. The history between the Savidges and Fleshers ran deep. But that didn't change the fact that they were all human. Humans made mistakes. Humans were also full of surprises.

"What's the game plan, then?" Spalding asked, eyeing the syringe.

Alastor slipped the syringe into his coat and cupped it with his hand. "We'll knock on the door, ask if they have any tools we can use for our carriage."

"Because it broke down," Spalding said, playing along.

"Correct," Alastor said. "We left it a couple blocks down and are hoping some kind folk would be willing to help us."

"That's when you use that poison of yours," Spalding said.

"Exactly. Whoever answers the door gets it first. If it is the man, perfect. If the wife answers, we'll ambush the husband together."

Spalding nodded. The plan was legitimate. Well, it was as convincing as a plan could be when it came to murder.

The two waited for a few more minutes in silence. There wasn't much to say at the moment. Spalding ran the scenario through his mind. He could already feel the adrenaline buzz through his hands. This pre-action energy spike wasn't like when he was at the fight club. No. This was something else entirely.

Spalding stared up at the streetlight directly above them. It was purely electrical, one of those arc lights he had little knowledge of. It fascinated him. A streetlight that operated entirely without gas. Entering the big city was always a thrill. With the turn of the century the technology, the fashion, and the culture evolved far faster than in a small town such as Rowley.

A part of Spalding wondered why they lived out in Rutherford Manor and not in a big city. Then he remembered the deep history that the home had that the families treasured. They belonged there. Plus, it wasn't exactly an easy option to up and leave to a city and buy a new home. Their families also had complex issues that made them outsiders. Outsiders that had no hope in hell of fitting in with society. They could only blend in. They were chameleons.

"Okay," Alastor said. "Let's not waste more time. The sooner we have them, the sooner we can wait for the White Hand."

Spalding and Alastor walked side by side down the street leading to the house. Spalding could feel his heart beat with every step that they made. This was it. Showtime.

Alastor approached the sizeable brown door first, raising his hand and knocking several times. The sound it created was thick and heavy. A type of noise that Alastor always made, whether it was talking, walking, or something with his hands. The man had a booming presence.

The door swung open, and a shorter, stocky man appeared in the doorway. His dark eyes scanned both newcomers before he said, "Can'ah help you?" His accent was thick, possibly Italian.

"Yes." Alastor cleared his throat. "We're in a bit of trouble, you see?"

"Yes?" the man said while shifting his stance.

Spalding took his eyes off the man's pencil mustache and glanced down both sides of the street. It was empty. All was good.

"Our carriage broke down, and we're hoping that someone would be able to help us with some tools."

"Whaddaya need?" the man asked.

"We need. . . ." Alastor paused, extending the vowels of the word *need*. He was stalling.

Before Alastor or Spalding could finish the sentence, a loud

"*HOO!*" erupted from above. The sound of fluffing feathers filled the air as a grey ball soared directly down, past the entrance, and into the home.

"What-dah?" the man said, turning around.

Alastor lunged forward, extending his syringe-holding hand into the man's neck. His other hand grabbed the man by the mouth, keeping him in place. With his one thumb, he pressed on the syringe, injecting the liquid into the man's body.

The man coughed a few times, arms flailing, trying to grab hold of Alastor.

Spalding slipped in, avoiding the wild arms, and examined the entrance. There was no one in immediate view. The foyer had pillars, marble flooring, an etched ceiling. The home was high-class.

Who are these people? Spalding thought.

Alastor shoved the man forward, pushing both of them into the home. His hair covered a part of his face as he struggled to maintain control of the victim. The two thrashed for dominance only for a couple of moments until the short man's energy began to decrease.

Spalding hurried and closed the door as the man continued to produce muffled groans.

A louder scream erupted. The sound didn't come from the man; it came from deeper inside the house.

Spalding and Alastor glanced over to see a young lady, wide-eyed in fear, watching them from the hallway leading to the kitchen.

"Grab her!" Alastor ordered.

Spalding dashed forward as the lady attempted to run to the

staircase that led to the second floor. He cut her off before she could make it, snagging her left forearm. The lady was frail in comparison to Spalding.

He lunged forward, grabbing her left arm. She let out a shriek as he spun her around. She lashed her right hand at him, nails slicing into his face. He grabbed her right hand, feeling her pointy three-spiked ring dig into his palm, holding her with both arms.

He ignored the small irritations and adjusted his arms swiftly, letting go of her forearms and snagging her mouth and neck. "Make any moves, and I will break your neck," he said.

The lady refused to listen and lunged her elbows into Spalding's chest, twice.

"Now you're pissing me off," Spalding said. He spun her around and coiled a fist, throwing it into the lady's face. The blow knocked her back. He threw another fist, this one hitting her in the jaw, sending her tumbling to the ground. Blood spilled from her lip as her face collided with the marble. Red liquid splattered from her mouth.

A thud came from the entrance as Alastor dropped the man. He held the empty syringe, looking down at the now unconscious victim below him. The short man's eyes were wide open. Nox's poison had worked its magic.

"Mom! Dad!" came a shout from the adjacent room.

Alastor looked over to see a boy was sitting in a chair with a book in hand. The living room. How did they miss the large area with a child? The lady's screams had to have overpowered Spalding's and Alastor's senses.

Alastor rushed towards the kid, pulling out a switchblade

from his pocket. He still held onto the syringe with the other hand.

The kid let out a scream and leaped from the chair, attempting to run past Alastor, who swung at him. His blade sliced into the kid's face, but not enough to knock him off-balance. The kid dashed over to the front door and tried to twist the knob open.

Alastor hacked at him again, missing him.

The kid screamed and rushed towards the kitchen, away from Spalding.

"Get him!" Alastor shouted.

Spalding hurried down the hallway, leading to the second entrance to the kitchen and cut the kid off. The boy was wide-eyed, a trait shared with his mother.

"HOO!" came a sound from the kitchen as a grey feathered ball soared down between the boy and Spalding. The interference gave the boy enough time to dart from the hallway entrance and towards the door leading to the backyard.

The owl fluttered away, allowing Spalding to chase the kid. The boy flung the door open and sprinted out across the backyard. Too late.

Shit, Spalding thought, watching as the kid leaped over a fence, disappearing into the night. There was no way Spalding could outrun that energized, fear-infused child.

"Did you get him?" Alastor shouted.

Spalding closed the door and looked around the room to see the owl perched on the chandelier, staring at him.

"Spalding?" Alastor asked while entering the kitchen.

"No," Spalding said.

"What the hell happened?"

Spalding pointed at the bird, saying, "Something got in the way."

"Damned animal," Alastor muttered. "That's okay. We got what we wanted."

"The boy saw our faces, though," Spalding said.

A knock came from the door. Both men tensed up. Who could it be? The police? How? Spalding felt the sweat on his skin turn to ice. Now they were victims of the unknown.

CHAPTER 7

BACKSTORY

There is something to be said about improvisation. You can discover new perspectives and opportunities that you might not have thought about previously. The only problem with spontaneous choice is that you leave yourself open to the risk of the unknown. Spontaneous action was the reverse of planning. Planning is a crucial component of making sure any given task is a success. A plan helps to create consistency.

Goddamnit, Spalding thought as he looked at the door, then to Alastor.

Another knock jolted them.

"Who the hell is that?" Alastor whispered.

Spalding shook his head. "How should I know? The mother and kid were screaming at the top of their lungs. Anyone could have heard it." He was frazzled. Rightfully so; the scenario had gone south fast. Anyone with a sense of sanity would be shaken up. That was something worth normality points.

"I'll answer it," Alastor said.

"What are you going to say?" Spalding asked.

Alastor marched towards the front door. He didn't reply. It was a typical move when he was under pressure. That irritating tendency not to include Spalding in the decision-making.

"Alastor!" Spalding called out.

The man stopped in his footsteps and looked back at him. "Yes?" he said.

"The body," Spalding said while rushing to join him.

Alastor looked down to see the short Italian man was right in the front lobby. The two grabbed the paralyzed man by the arms and dragged him out of view. Spalding hurried to the woman and took her around the corner.

Another knock from the door erupted.

Alastor brushed his hair from his face, took a deep breath, and walked calmly to the door. Opening it, he said, "Hello?"

Spalding could make out an elderly man at the door who took his hat off in respect and made a slight bow. "Good evening, sorry to trouble you. I was just on my walk and heard some sounds. Horrific sounds from your home. Is everything alright?"

"HOO!" the owl hooted as it soared down from the chandelier in the kitchen, and towards the front door.

Alastor ducked as the animal flew outside.

"Heavens!" the old man said.

Alastor stood up and shook his head. "That was causing us a lot of grief. The damned animal got inside while we were returning home."

"Chaos." The old man waved at Alastor. "I am glad to hear that everything is okay."

"Thank you for your concern. Goodnight," Alastor said as he closed the door.

Spalding let out a sigh of relief while reaching for a cigarette. "Close one," he said while lighting the smoke and taking a puff.

"That owl turned out to be a blessing in disguise," Alastor muttered. He walked over to the unconscious woman and pulled out his knife. "We don't have enough of the solution for her. That fat lard took it all."

Spalding puffed on his cigarette. He knew where this was going. They would have to kill her in cold blood. The question was, what was the best way to stage a natural death? "What do you propose?" Spalding asked.

"We break her neck," Alastor said while getting down on his knees and grabbing hold of the lady. "Easy enough to do."

"You do that. I'll make sure we didn't leave any clues before we close this place up." Spalding walked around to the kitchen and examined the room. It was simple, high-quality craftsmanship. The running boards were all carved and painted with impressive detail. Then there was that gold-plated chandelier. Good taste in furnishings, much like the marble flooring. These people were someone, but who?

The kitchen offered no clues to the mystery. A candle snuffer was on the counter beside a set of knives. Casually, Spalding grabbed the snuffer and extinguished the candles in the chandelier, leaving the room in darkness. Onward. The hallway was crowded with beautiful paintings mounted on the walls. There were even a few photographs too. The photos appeared to be of family members, possibly the first generation to enter America. Impossible to identify.

A snap echoed through the quiet house. The deed was done. Spalding hadn't wanted to end the poor woman's life. She was nothing but a victim of the cruel reality that the Fleshers and Savidges found themselves in.

Spalding moved through the dining room, around to the half-closed door. The light was on. Curiosity roared through him. He cautiously opened the door, causing the old wood to creak as it swayed aside. Bookshelves lined the walls. A table and chair were on the far end. A candle was on the desk as well. Curtains covered the window.

Someone was doing something here, Spalding thought. He stepped into the room, looking at the bookshelves. Without a doubt, this was the study. Reaching the table, he could see a black ink bottle and several sheets of paper on the surface. One of them was half complete with a large black hand on the center of the page. A couple of daggers were also illustrated beside the text. Stencils rested beside the ink bottle, half dry, half wet.

Spalding put his smoke into his mouth and flipped the paper over. He read the handwritten text below the illustration. The handwriting was nondecorated, etch style—a tactic commonly used to hide one's identity. The letter read:

ONE WEEK. PAY UP. GREEDY WHORE.

~ BLACK HAND.

Friendly, Spalding thought while putting the letter down. A black-ink-covered paper peeked from under the stack of blank sheets. He pulled the paper out from under the others to see a familiar white hand in the middle of the sheet. On the flip side was more etched-style writing. It read:

DONNIE,

WE OWE YOU NOTHING. BACK OFF OR YOU'RE NEXT.

~ WHITE HAND.

Gang dispute, Spalding thought. "Alastor!" Spalding called out. He took his cigarette out of his mouth, pressing it into the table to extinguish it. He felt his face begin to tighten, sculpting stress on his expression, as realization dawned on him.

Alastor stepped into the room and walked up to join him at the desk. "What is it?" he asked.

"Look," Spalding said, passing him the letter. "Donnie was the man we killed. He had a response letter too."

Alastor looked over the letter and muttered, "Shit."

"The Black Hand, Alastor!" Spalding said. "The Italian mob."

"I know who they are, Spalding."

"We gotta slow things down. Why didn't we just get the old man?"

"Because a young lady has more value!"

Spalding pressed on his eyebrows. "I know. We need to screen people better. This is an amateur move."

Alastor sighed and looked around the room. "That explains the decor of their digs."

"Of course it does," Spalding returned. He blew out the candle and walked out of the room. Their whole tactic was reckless. They were idiotic for not planning. Spalding couldn't believe that they had gotten themselves into a deeper mess than they were already in. A much, much deeper mess.

Alastor followed him out of the room. "This isn't all bad," he said. "No one knows we were here. We selected them at random. There's no way they can trace this back to us."

"Perhaps, or perhaps the Black Hand will think the White Hand did this. What if Bran recognizes these two?"

"He won't. We'll only hand over the woman."

"Planning, Alastor!" Spalding said. "This resurrectionist business is making you blind."

"Yes, Spalding!" Alastor snapped. "It is making me blind. Do you know why?"

Spalding turned to face him. "You're rushing into this."

"Because I'm old, Spalding. Money isn't good for us. You think Nox is ready to become head of the family? No! We need money. I need to spend more time with Nox and less time chasing scraps. Do you have any idea of the depths that I have gone to try and get us above water?"

"Aye, I have, mostly. You tend to be a little secretive at times, which is a piss-off."

"I keep you in the dark for your own protection! I don't think you have the spirit to handle some of these unholy things I've tried." Alastor stepped closer to him. "This agreement with the White Hand will let us buy food. Then we don't have to keep eating people!"

Cannibalism—the grim secret of Rutherford Manor. The real truth that separated the Fleshers and Savidges from everyone else. No one knew, of course, but eating people had a way of changing the way you see the world and interact with others.

It wasn't like Spalding didn't know about their behaviour before. Everyone at the manor knew. No one really wanted to talk about the repulsive act. It was only a survival tactic. Hearing Alastor say it out loud was like a stone-cold fist of reality to the face. Worse than making a bad swing at the fight club.

Spalding looked at the dead woman, then over to the paralyzed man. *I wonder if he can hear anything?* was the odd thought that entered his mind. It didn't really matter, though. That chum was on a one-way ticket to his grave.

"Spalding," Alastor said. "I don't mean to be harsh. But when you get to my old age, cannibalism and time away from your son isn't exactly what you want to be doing. So, forgive me if I am a little reckless to move things along faster. This resurrectionist work is the first good thing to happen to us in years."

"It's not like you, that is all," Spalding said.

"You're right. Perhaps all of this has rattled up a deeper hunger in me. A primal one. I did feel blindsided today. Possibly the most I ever have." Alastor walked over to the paralyzed man. "I'm too old for this."

Spalding put his hands on his hips. "Alastor, forgive me for losing my temper. I understand your frustration."

"Do you?" Alastor said.

Spalding paused. He wasn't sure how much of his inner conflict he should share with Alastor. His lack of a wife and a skewed moral compass were the hauntings of his mind. It was a lot to share and would probably take a lot more time than they had. *Forget it,* he thought.

"I certainly do not enjoy eating such taboo meals myself," Spalding said. "It's probably a silent agreement among everyone at the manor." Spalding patted Alastor on the shoulder. "We got our snatch. Let's deliver this to Bran so we can get paid. Maybe more than last time, hey?"

Keep cool and collected, Spalding thought. *That is what we need right now.* Whether he liked it or not, they were now in this mess of body-snatching.

"Thank you, Spalding," Alastor said. "You truly are your father's son."

"We're business partners," Spalding said with a smirk.

"We're also friends. I couldn't keep the Flesher name alive if it weren't for the Savidges. Your father would be proud."

Spalding tipped his hat to Alastor. "Kind words. Now, let's finish up. Shall I get the carriage?"

"Please. I'll clean up here," Alastor said.

"Good. Next time, no families."

Alastor chuckled. "Agreed. I should have listened to you."

Let's get the hell out of this place. Spalding thought. It was the second snatch on their job and they were making significant leeway into their personal lives. Who needed a priest to confess to when you could just kill people and reveal your deepest concerns to your friends? So far, it was pretty effective.

CHAPTER 8

DELIVERY

Spalding fetched the carriage from back at the marketplace as Alastor cleaned up the home. The night streets seemed to be clear, but Alastor asked, just to be sure. He was paranoid considering that they were in a Black Hand home and the child had gotten away. Spalding confirmed that they were still alone. Good. People in the big city were too busy in their own lives to really pay attention to some strangers with a carriage. Spalding took it around to the back of the house so they could load up a couple of indiscreet, rolled-up, lumpy sacks. They placed the woman on top and kept the man hidden underneath some additional sacks and out of sight.

Spalding brought the skull-decorated cane into the house as they extinguished the remaining lights. *Disgusting,* Alastor thought. Spalding, the man with a strange sense of honour. The two wiped up all the blood and exited the home. They left the belongings as they were. They weren't about to get caught with stolen goods from deceased members of the Black Hand. They had to minimize evidence of their presence in the house.

Alastor and Spalding sat in the front of the carriage, lighting the lantern, as their horse trotted along the streets, leading them to the planned rendezvous.

"Another pay," Alastor said. "Another day closer to a real life." *Until it is time,* came a wispy voice. The same voice that lingered in the back of his mind constantly. He wondered if this was all a mistake. He could only pray the price was worth the sacrifice.

"Aye," Spalding said. "Some bacon sure would be good for breakfast."

"We'll have to look into that," Alastor said. *We'll get through this,* he thought. *We always do.* The body-snatching wasn't what was concerning. Killing was so natural to him. It was his own energy levels that were a worry. He couldn't do business and raise a family at the same time. That was why he'd had a life partner, his dear wife.

A flash of her hazelnut eyes and white smile entered his mind. Her soft, feminine smell flew through his memories. The type of scent he hadn't experienced in years. How he missed her so. Matilda was nothing more than a memory, a thought that lived in his mind. Folks were kind and had reminded him that her soul had moved on. She was now with God in heaven. Alastor wasn't so sure. The Fleshers weren't saints.

Spalding and Alastor reached the outskirts of Chicago and their familiar meeting place at the top of the hill. The long grass blew in the wind, déjà vu to the last meeting they'd had with the White Hand. Unlike last time, the White Hand were already here. The Black Hand surprise had set the resurrectionists off-schedule.

"Alastor," came Bran's deep voice.

Alastor brought the carriage to a stop and waved at the man. He was as well dressed as last time and had two henchmen with him. There was the familiar long-haired fellow and there was what seemed to be a *henchwoman* with him replacing one of the goons. Alastor could barely tell at first with her face underneath that hat.

That'll get Spalding drooling, Alastor thought. He couldn't help but smile for a split second at the amusing visual of his partner with a chin covered in saliva.

Alastor cleared his throat, saying, "you must forgive us for being late."

Bran stepped forward. "What was the holdup? We're busy."

Alastor and Spalding hopped off the carriage and approached the group. Spalding unhooked the lantern to provide light.

"We had a bit of a delay. Nothing to worry about, though," Alastor said. *A lie if I ever knew one,* he thought. He couldn't believe that he'd been foolish enough to just charge in and take the family. They'd screened the farmer carefully last time, made sure he wasn't going to be missed. Who knew, with any luck maybe the Black Hand wouldn't read into Donnie or his wife now missing.

"Shall we take you to the goods?" Spalding asked. He eyed all three of the White Hand members. His gaze stopped on the mysterious new lady. Typical of Spalding.

"Please," Bran said.

The five walked around to the back of the carriage and Alastor unlocked it, opening the back door and revealing a

The White Hand by Konn Lavery

neatly wrapped body in canvas.

"Blyton," Bran said.

The White Hand henchman stepped forward and unravelled the canvas to reveal a woman's pale face.

"A woman?" Bran said with excitement. "A rather young one too."

Blyton pressed his hand against her neck. "She's recently deceased," he said.

Bran turned to face Alastor. They were eye-level; the White Hand member was one of the few men equal to his own height. Even though Bran was thinner, the man was intimidating. He carried himself with a level of confidence that made Alastor a bit uneasy to be near him. Hell, the dead were less threatening to have around.

"Impressive work, gentlemen," Bran said.

He doesn't know her, Alastor thought. He felt a wave of relief rush over him. "Thank you," he said.

"Let's get you paid, shall we?" Bran said while taking a step towards Alastor. "Blyton, Irene, take care of this."

Alastor leaned closer to Spalding, saying, "Mind giving them a hand? I'll grab the payment, see if we can squeeze a bit more. Then we can get out of here."

"Sure," Spalding said, keeping his eye on the woman.

Bran and Alastor walked away from the carriage towards the White Hand members' horses.

"Alastor, you do impress me," Bran said.

"Thank you. I am glad to offer prime specimens."

"Share with me—this couldn't have been your ideal line of work. What got you into the resurrectionist business?"

"At the moment, we don't have a lot of options. We have mouths to feed, and this is our best bet. I could ask you the same thing about being a member of the White Hand."

"True enough," Bran chuckled. "You said mouths to feed. You have a family?"

Too many questions, Alastor thought. He liked their previous black-and-white business relations. It appeared Bran wanted to associate himself more with Alastor now that they had provided two quality bodies. Perhaps the plan of exceeding expectations had backfired. Alastor didn't want the White Hand to know more about his family. Especially after he'd murdered members of the Black Hand.

"I do," he said. "I have two sons and a daughter. Well, one son is no longer with us." *Small lie. Walter.*

"I'm terribly sorry. I have two sons myself and Irene over there," Bran said.

"She's your daughter?" Alastor asked.

"Yes, she is a tough one. She'd put most men under her boot if I let her."

Alastor laughed. "A heart for violence. I can relate to that quite well with my family's affairs."

"It appears we're not so different after all. What does your son do?"

"He was at the University of Chicago for a while until he came back to us."

"Recently?"

"Yes," Alastor said.

"My son goes there as well. Bright young boy. The youngest of the two. I've kept him out of the family business so he can pursue other values."

"I wish I could say the same for mine. Unfortunately, there was an accident, and he was physically damaged. We had to bring him home."

"Terrible news," Bran said.

"Indeed," Alastor said. "But now we can take care of him. Well, I can. My wife passed away, and it is just myself and my business partner."

"It's like looking into the mirror," Bran muttered.

"I beg your pardon?" Alastor asked.

"My wife is no longer with me either. She died a few years back."

"My condolences. We have more in common than we thought."

"It appears so. I take it you're a family man? Based on the lengths you are willing to go to ensure that they have something to eat and a roof over their heads."

"Yes, family is above all."

"I couldn't agree more," Bran said. "Let's get you gentlemen paid." Bran walked over to his horse and unzipped the saddle pouch. He pulled out a lumpy bag and handed it over to Alastor. "As before, it is all there."

Alastor peeked inside the bag to double-check. Indeed, there were stacks of paper in there. The green demon. The small, simple thing that drove him to do these dark acts. The abstract concept of money was a funny one. Here he was, a man who put his values on family first, but was obsessed over cold, lifeless pieces of paper.

"Thank you," Alastor said. "Now, I have a proposal for you."

"Yes?" Bran asked.

"How about we introduce price brackets for the type of bodies that we can provide you. Surely a youthful lady is worth more than an old gizzard."

Bran folded his arms. "You have proven to offer high-quality corpses. I must say, the anatomist that we brought the last corpse to was beyond excited when he saw how fresh that corpse was."

"That is worth something," Alastor said.

"Okay, we can work out a pricing," Bran said.

"How about for this current one?"

Bran stood silent for several moments.

Come on, Alastor thought.

Bran nodded. "Okay." He reached into his pocket and pulled out some cash, handing it over to Alastor. "You aren't just a resurrectionist, are you?"

"Nope," Alastor said while taking the cash. It wasn't much more, but it was something. "Like you said, this was not my first choice. Same time next week?" Alastor asked, pocketing the money.

"Of course," Bran said while extending his hand.

Alastor shook it firmly and attempted to let go, but Bran did not.

"One thing, Alastor."

Alastor looked him in the eyes. Bran returned the stare. The two did not lose contact.

"I do like you, Alastor. However, do not ever confuse my personal interactions with naivety. If you ever conceive the idea of double-crossing me, I will kill you and your family." Bran let go of his hand.

Alastor stared at him for a few seconds before saying, "Of course. I would expect nothing less. As I would to you."

Bran raised an eyebrow. "Then we really are reflections." He looked over to the carriage and waved at the three who stood at the back. "Let's move!"

Blyton and Spalding took hold of the now covered body and hauled it over to the three horses. The two men grunted as they lifted the body up and onto one of the saddles.

Spalding wiped his hands and nodded at Irene as she walked by. Her red locks bounced up and down as she passed him.

Alastor patted Spalding on the arm. "Stay clear of her. It's not worth the trouble. Let's head home."

He felt a wave of relief rush over him. The task was done. They had the money and could move on to a cleaner snatch next week. Each snatch they concluded lifted a small amount of weight off of Alastor's back. The stress and the fear of survival was slowly dissolving. There was a promising future for Rutherford Manor. The risk would be worth the reward. Soon, there would be no more eating people, no more evil, no more sacrifices, and no more shady deals. They would survive.

At the price of our agreement.

CHAPTER 9

IN THE NAME OF SCIENCE

Fate: a concept that implies that you have no control over your choices and everything has been predefined on an inevitable path. There is nothing you can do to change the course of events. Fate is also believed to be the work of God, hence why no man is able to intervene. 'God works in mysterious ways,' as people like to say. Is that really so? God has a funny way of showing that to those who have done right. He also has an odd affinity for blessing those that have no chance of ever redeeming themselves.

If fate is true, it is not always a bad thing, either. On the contrary, it can be positive. There can be a series of events that lead to something uplifting or to someone elevating who can change your world. Sometimes these dualities of good and bad cross over to such a degree that you wonder if they are really one and the same. Maybe there is no right or wrong to fate. Perhaps we only describe events as fate to make sense of a string of random circumstances. Fate has nothing to do with anything, meaning God is not present. God is never present because he only lives in the minds of men and women.

This was a logical rationalization. Or at least it was a better explanation than 'the work of God' when it came to the unexplainable. Chaos. Nothing but pure chaos in a vast void of what we call reality.

"It will heal. We will find a way to fix it," came a soft voice of a girl. She stared at the boy beside her with bright blue eyes as they sat in chairs in the dark room. A glimmer of light shined through the circular window, casting sharp shadows against the two figures.

"N-n-n-o, Lilith," Nox said as he looked away from her. He knew she was trying to be encouraging to him, tell him that everything was going to work out. He knew it couldn't. It was impossible for him to be the boy he once was before.

"We will try," Lilith said while shifting her seat to face him. "I've been working on some remedies. Testing them, of course, but I believe we can try."

Nox sighed. "Th-th-thank you. I really don't th-th-think it will ever heal, though. This is me now." The words hit his heart heavy. Maybe even as heavy as the explosion that had melted the flesh in the first place. What a foolish mistake. Acid. Something that you shouldn't leave on a burner.

"I was s-s-so stupid," Nox said.

"It wasn't your fault!" Lilith said.

"It was my equipment. My experiment. M-m-my mistake. I was so stupid."

"I still care for you," Lilith said, taking the boy's hand. Her hand was soft and warm, complementing her soothing smell. "I know you are upset," she said. "You have every right to be. But you are alive. This didn't kill you, and you still have so much more to offer this world. So much more to offer your family!"

Kind words, he thought. He had to say thank you. He wanted to tell Lilith that she was a light in his life. No words came out of him, though. Instead, the boy locked up. Silence was typical for him, even before the acid mangled his face. Nox wasn't like other kids. He was more interested in spending time alone in his study.

It baffled him that there was so much left undiscovered in this world. He blamed people's foolish attempts to justify everything with God. He was painfully aware of how little humans knew about the stars or the way our bodies worked. Nox wanted to find out more. He also had an unnatural way of dreaming up schematics, the level of skill that others only dream of. Kind of like the way he imagined what life would be like if he was less dense when it came to social etiquette. People weren't like his projects. They had emotions and were unpredictable.

"I'm here with you," Lilith said while stroking his hand. It was a calming feeling.

"Th-th-th-thank you," Nox finally managed to say. *That's all I have?* he thought. It amazed him that Lilith was so willing to be with him. The girl truly cared about him, yet he didn't fully understand why. Perhaps she did speak the truth and appreciated him for who he was and not the hideous monstrosity he'd turned into.

A knock came from the door, causing the two to perk up.

"Come in," Lilith said.

The door opened, and Alastor walked in. He took long strides, hands in his pockets. "Hello, Lilith. Nox," he said.

"Mr. Flesher," Lilith said.

"F-f-father," Nox said. "What ca-ca-can I do for you?"

Alastor grinned. "Remember that pigeon of yours?"

"Y-yes," Nox said.

"Well, I have something that might be of interest to you. Please, come with me."

Lilith and Nox exchanged glances, then the boy stood up. His hand slid from hers, leaving the warmth of her body. Only the cold air surrounded him now.

"You must excuse us, Lilith," Alastor said with a bow. "We shan't be too long."

"No hurry," Lilith said.

Nox got up from his seat and followed his father out of the study, returning down to the main floor of Rutherford Manor. His father continued to lead him around the staircase and to the basement.

"Wh-wh-where are we going, Father?" Nox asked.

"I was quite pleased with what you and Lilith managed to conjure up for Spalding and me. It worked amazingly well," he said in a wicked tone.

Father rarely got this excited. Nox knew he and Lilith must have provided something of value. This was good.

"Th-th-thank you, Father," Nox said. "I am glad to hear that it worked for you. How much did you use?"

"Well, all of it. The target was a bit large, and it took a while for the solution to go throughout his body. Once it settled in, the man was as limp as that bird."

The two reached the bottom of the stairs. Alastor unlocked the door and pushed it open, stepping into the basement.

"Wh-what is down here?" Nox asked. He'd known about the basement while growing up, but never had the opportunity to explore it. It was usually locked.

"As you know, I used to spend a lot of time down here when your mother was alive," Alastor said.

"Yes," Nox said. A brief memory of his mother flashed before his eyes. He didn't have a lot of visuals of her. More so a feeling. Like the feeling of warmth and love. Motherly love, an emotion that is unmatched.

"Of course," Alastor said, "after we lost her to the will of God, I had to shift my priorities, and this place has been primarily unused."

A spark of light burst from a lantern that Alastor held. The lamplight revealed the open basement of Rutherford Manor. There was plenty of shelving space, a large chest, a table, and a chair in the space. Two hallways led in opposite directions, deeper into the dungeon.

"Nox, welcome to your new study," Alastor said.

"My study?" Nox asked.

"Yes, everything down here is now yours. Please, go on, explore." Alastor handed Nox the lantern.

Nox's eyes widened. His father had just passed him his old study. It was like an honorarium, no, a promotion. Nox felt like this could really be his effort to contribute to the family. He gripped the lantern excitedly and stepped deeper into one of the halls.

His steps echoed with each move he made. There were a

couple of closed doors in the hall. So many entries, so many rooms. This dungeon was littered with opportunities. He could run multiple experiments at once!

Nox entered another room; this one was much larger and contained extinguished lanterns from the ceiling. Chains, hooks, and rope hung from the support beams.

Rattling echoed from the darkness, catching Nox's attention.

A hand gently landed on Nox's shoulder. He looked back to see his father was beside him.

"Go on," his father said.

Nox walked forward, keeping the lantern light high, casting a yellow hue deeper into the room. The light gradually revealed a pair of feet. They twitched. Then ankles. They were strapped to an angled operating table by leather. Then there were legs. Further up was the torso of a large round man. His eyes were closed, arms strapped to his sides.

"Wh-wh-who is this?" Nox asked.

"The catch that Spalding and I made during our last snatch," Alastor said as he walked towards the man. "We applied the solution to him that you made; it worked quite well. However, he still twitches once in a while."

"It wasn't perfect then," Nox muttered.

"No, not everything is. But it served its purpose, and we were able to finish the job. So, think of this basement as your reward for providing an excellent solution."

"Thank you, Father." Nox said while stepping closer to the paralyzed man. He examined his eyes, hands, and chest. The man was still breathing, barely, but he was alive. "How long has he been this way?"

"Since last night. Spalding and I got back home quite early this morning. I must admit, I am tired. Shall I leave you to your new study?"

"Of course. F-f-feel free to do as you need, Father," Nox said.

"Good. Enjoy," Alastor said as he walked past his son.

"Father, wait."

"Yes?"

"Why is this man here?" Nox had a hunch as to why his dad brought him a paralyzed man to the bottom of the basement. He knew why the man was strapped to the operating table and why his father took him down to the old study.

I just want to hear him say it, Nox thought. Hearing his father's words of permission would be the cherry on top. The finalization.

"Well, you've been working with animals throughout your life, haven't you?" Alastor asked.

"Yes, I've l-l-learned quite a bit."

"You have. Vivisections are a challenging task. Most specimens die within moments upon the surgery. You've been quite successful with it to date. I know you've wanted to expand your studies. So, this is your first project."

Nox smiled. It was a genuine expression of excitement. He didn't smile a lot—especially now—and when he did, it actually made his facial skin feel uncomfortable because the response was so rare for him. This was a special occasion, and cause for the face-stretch of joy.

"Get your tools, son," Alastor said.

"I will. I'll continue my studies and of-f-fer something truly unique to the family," Nox said.

"I know you will."

Nox took a bow before his father left him to his new study.

His father believed in him. This was finally the time for Nox to contribute to the business. He could improve upon the solution. He could do better. All he needed to do was see people on the inside. See what made them tick.

ACT II

Anger

CHAPTER 10

RUMBLE REWARD

Snowflakes fell over the dark sky seen through frosted glass. It was the kind of night where you want to stay indoors by a fire, cuddled up close to those you care about. Those that have continuously been in your life. This was the type of night for peace, silence, and relaxation. Well, not for everyone. Not if you have no loved ones and you find yourself outside. The cold can make you bitter and grumpy. Especially if you need to travel a significant distance just to get to where you need to go.

Damned winter, Spalding thought as he hugged his coat to him with one hand and tied his horse to the post with the other. It wasn't like he had to go out. He could have easily stayed at Rutherford Manor and watched the snow fall from the warmth of his home. You know, normal people things.

Instead, he was out here, about to get his brawl on. He couldn't help it. The fight club was the one thing that he was able to do for himself. Even though it changed locations often, it was a regular feature in Spalding's life. His therapy. It was the one constant in life. Sure, there had been other temporary consistencies such as the recent resurrectionist business. But Spalding was always skeptical of them and stayed on his toes. He made sure he didn't get too comfortable in one thing. Life had a funny way of changing. For all he knew, the resurrectionist business could end tomorrow. Hell, it had only been a few months since they'd gotten involved. A few beautiful months of not having to resort to cannibalism. So, things were looking up for him.

Thankfully, to date, they hadn't heard anything about their second snatching gig. The snatch that had caused both Spalding and Alastor to snap. The Black Hand didn't contact them, and the White Hand didn't appear to have any related trouble that they knew of. Perhaps they were in the clear.

That Irene gal, Spalding thought. He'd seen her a few times when he and Alastor delivered bodies to the White Hand. She appeared more frequently than Niles as of late. Blyton and Bran were the regulars. *How I'd like to see what type of secrets she keeps under the sheets.* The girl had a rare attraction. Irene wasn't like other gals. She was a mobster.

Spalding finished tying his horse to the post and hurried over to the barn. Lights were on at the top of the structure; that meant fights were happening. He hurried over to the side door, wanting to get inside and out of the cold as soon as possible. He reached the door only to have it burst open in front of him. A large burly man with a black ponytail emerged outside.

Billy. "Evening!" Spalding said.

"Goodnight," Billy said in a cold tone as he walked by him.

"Leaving so soon? But I just got here."

"Too bad."

"We haven't had ourselves a match yet!" Spalding called out.

"Another time," Billy said as he waved goodbye.

Strange fellow, Spalding thought. Then again, considering the troubles the man encountered due to his ethnicity, he didn't blame Billy for giving people the cold shoulder. Billy was an outcast.

Spalding snagged the closing door and stepped in. The inside of the barn wasn't much better than the outside. There were a couple of caged fires burning, which helped, but they didn't produce enough heat to warm the whole place. It looked like Spalding would have to warm his blood up with a few fists.

He wandered throughout the barn to see if he could spot any familiar faces. There were a couple he knew, mostly from fights or chewing the fat, so he gave them a wave and a tilt of his hat.

I need a drink, he thought. *That will warm me up.*

Considering the new location of the fight club wasn't a bar, and it was the beginning of winter, there was no liquor on tap of any kind. The fight club changed locations frequently to keep the law on their toes. The promoters knew who the regulars were and who they could trust to spread the word of the new spot. Spalding was one of those entrusted folk, but he didn't bother informing other people of the news. The White Hand kept him busy enough. He wasn't an open book. Regarding the booze, thankfully, he'd thought ahead. Spalding was a Savidge, after all. Planning was their preferred method of action. He reached into his inner coat pocket and pulled out a flask, taking a shot of whiskey.

"Evening, Spalding!" came a manly voice.

Spalding looked over to see a familiar mustached man. Jacob. "Aye! How are you doing, bloke?" Spalding said, shaking the man's hand.

"A flask? You always think ahead, my friend," Jacob said with a smile.

"Once I caught wind that this place was going to be out in the middle of nowhere, I figured I had to come prepared," Spalding said. "Who sets up a fight club in a barn in winter?"

Jacob shrugged. "It is a bit chilly, isn't it? Perhaps the basement of the hotel is busy tonight. It happens."

"Apparently. I wish the fight club stuck to one location, you know? It'd make things a lot easier, like when it's cold."

"Well, it's better to keep the law on their toes. You can only pay them off to look away so much."

"True to that."

"I'm going to go watch Smith's fight with Alex. Maybe place a bet."

Spalding raised his flask at Jacob. He didn't know who the two men Jacob mentioned were and didn't care to find out. He eyed the room; it was primarily the usual hardcore crowd that came out for a show, which meant fewer new women. Unfortunate.

His eyes landed on a dark-haired man standing near the back of the barn by one of the caged fires. Niles. His arms folded, staring at the flame. His right hand rested on his forearm, exposing the three-spiked ring.

Strange, Spalding thought, narrowing his eyes at Niles' focus on the fire. *Plenty of other things to look at here.* As if on cue, his attention perked up at the sight of a passing girl. Her breasts was pushed up from her corset underneath her fur coat. She held some towels, probably for a bloody fighter.

That rack! I need me a girl like that, Spalding thought. He took another shot of his whiskey and put the flask back into his coat pocket, walking towards the White Hand man.

Niles raised his head as Spalding arrived.

"Good evening, sir," Spalding said.

"Evening," Niles said coldly.

"You've been absent for a little while," Spalding said.

"What do you mean?" Niles asked.

"Here at the fight club. And I don't see you around as much with Bran."

"Well, I've had some personal issues that are clouding my mind. I've been on the downlow."

"Care to elaborate? We're not that close, but that's part of this place. It allows you to let your guard down, metaphorically."

"My love. She died during the summer," Niles said while covering the hand wearing the spiked ring.

"My condolences. What was her name?"

"Angeline," Niles said as he gazed back into the fire. "Beautiful mind and body. Something that you hear about in books and folktales. True love."

Spalding scratched his head. "Well, we all hear about those stories. I'm bold enough to leave them at that."

"What of you, Spalding?"

Spalding chuckled. "That is a common question. The answer is simple: there's just me."

"Take no offence, but at your age, you should be thinking about these things."

"I'm aware," Spalding said while going for his flask. *This kind of talk again.* It was frustrating enough with Alastor making jabs about Spalding's lack of marriage, but now Niles—a mobster—was providing life advice? It never seemed to end.

A slim figure approached the two of them, catching Spalding's attention. It was a lady, wearing trousers, an open long black trench coat, and a wide-brimmed hat. Strands of curly red hair dangled in front of emerald eyes.

Irene.

"This place is quite the dive, ain't it?" she said while eyeing Niles. She didn't even notice Spalding. Who did she think she was? Not often did a gal ignore him. This dame had her own agenda.

Niles shrugged at her. "Well, there isn't a lot of pickings here. I've been coming to these on and off for long enough now that I don't think we're going to have any luck. Chicago had better options. Hell, even bringing in White Hand members from New York to here is a better idea."

"Aye, we should tell Bran this isn't worth our time. The Black Hand have me on edge since Donnie's death and I need to shake the stress off."

Huh. Alastor and I did mess things up, Spalding thought, recalling the second snatch.

"Yeah," Niles said. "I think Donnie's boss will calm down. Thugs die all the time."

"Donnie wasn't just a thug, though. He had pull in Chicago."

"Not as much as we do. They will back off."

"Damn well hope so," Irene said. "That dispute is all I've been dealing with." She pulled out a smoke and lighter, igniting it.

The gal puffed a couple of times before looking over at Spalding.

Spalding tipped his hat. "Evening. It's been a while," he said.

"Evening. I take it you come here often?" Irene said.

"I take it you don't," Spalding said.

"Not of late," she said. Her eyes locked onto his. They were deep, like a bright void, if there was such a thing. Her complexion was highlighted from the fire, softening her freckles. She had similarities to her father, Bran, for sure. He was a handsome man. It would only make sense that he would have a daughter with banging good looks too.

"Yeah, well. . . ," Spalding said while adjusting his coat. *What do I say?* he thought. This girl was making him nervous. Why? Was it her natural beauty? Cold stare? Her choice to take control of her own life? Maybe one of these. Maybe it was all three—the trinity of his desires. *Say something funny.* Spalding thought for a moment. "The fight club is kind of my therapy."

Irene snorted. It was high-pitched, making the sound a hell of a lot cuter than that of a man or beast. She smiled at him, which amplified the dimple on her cheek. "Therapy? What kind of therapy is beating other people to show who is more physically dominant?"

"Hey, there's more to it than that," Spalding said.

Irene walked over to Spalding, a few feet away. She was a head shorter than him, but her confidence made her height equal to his. Seductive. "Elaborate then," she said.

"Well," Spalding said, "there's the betting aspect. Chump change, but it buys a drink."

"That's all, huh?"

"It shows manhood amongst each other. Grows bonds. You'd

be surprised how much you can learn from someone when you throw punches at each other."

"Really?" Irene asked. "So, the physical connection really brings you closer to them?"

"I guess you could say that."

"I know of a more interesting method of physical connection. . . ." She winked at him.

She flirting with me? Spalding thought. He knew it already but had to ask himself just to be sure. He wasn't used to having a woman come on to him this strong. Usually, there was more of a dance to the courtship.

"There is more than one way to bond with someone," Spalding said. "With a lady, I prefer to relate on a more . . . intimate level," he said with a smile.

"Lucky me," Irene said softly, not blinking while keeping eye contact with Spalding.

Niles coughed, breaking the intensity.

Spalding blinked a couple times. "I came here to have at least one friendly fight. May I excuse myself for a moment?" he asked.

Irene extended her hand to the crowd, not saying a word.

"A pleasure," Spalding said, tipping his hat at her before walking away.

Wow, Spalding thought. That gal wasn't anything that Spalding was expecting. He wanted to spend the rest of the night talking to her. Take her for a drink and a ride. Maybe he could make tonight a different kind of connection.

One fight, just to say I did because I'm here, Spalding thought. *Then I can see what kind of agenda Irene has.*

Spalding walked through the crowd for a few moments,

looking around to see if any blokes were looking to have themselves a go with him in the ring. There were three rings of people fighting. One was defined clearly with stones on the ground. The other two occupied rings were made up by a rim of people around them watching intensely. Usually, men looking to have an unscheduled brawl hung around the back.

A group of men sat against the corner of the barn watching the farthest ring. They chatted with each other quietly. Jacob was among them.

Spalding approached the men, walking beside Jacob.

"I thought you were going to watch Smith and Alex?" Spalding asked.

Jacob shrugged. "I caught the end of it, or the fight was really short. Didn't even get to bet."

"What a shame." Spalding walked in front of the group of four men. "Who wants to have a casual go?"

The four men exchanged looks at each other until one man stepped forward. He wore a white work shirt and suspenders. "I'll have one with ye," he said. His exaggerated Adam's apple bobbed up and down as he spoke.

Abnormally greasy hair. "Brilliant. What's your name?" Spalding extended his hand.

"Michael," the man said, shaking it. His handshake was weak. It was difficult to trust people that had weak handshakes. What made it so hard for them to have a solid grasp? Soft grasps were kind of rude too, Spalding reflected. Show some respect and firmly grip the man you are about to interact with.

"Spalding," he introduced himself. "I can't say I have had the honour of having a fight with you."

"Nor I. To be honest, this is my first time."

"First time here?" Spalding turned to the man, raising an eyebrow. "What the hell are you doing fighting me then?"

"I wanted to check it out. Prove myself. Figured I could learn a thing or two here."

"Well, that you will."

"Will people be taking bets?"

"Let's keep it to just us brawling, eh? It's your first go." *Maybe I should go easy on him,* Spalding thought. *Or perhaps I should destroy him. That would really teach him a lesson he wouldn't forget.*

The two walked side by side to the empty rock-lined ring.

Spalding took off his coat and tossed it to the side, then put his hat on top of it. He rolled up his sleeves and unbuttoned one button on his shirt. It was a little too cold to go bare-chested, but Spalding figured he might as well make himself as comfortable as he could when he was about to take a fist to the face.

Michael held up his arms, fists coiled with his head slightly lowered.

The two men in the ring caught the attention of nearby audience members and the ring was quickly surrounded by people eager to watch.

"Ready?" Spalding said.

"Aye," Michael replied with a nod.

Spalding brought his fists up and moved into a fighting position, stepping closer to the young man. The two shifted stances side by side for several moments, waiting for the other to make the first move. Spalding liked to dance a bit with his opponent before making his first swing. It kept them on edge.

Michael took the initiative and swung at him. His right hook was elongated and sloppy, easy enough to dodge.

Spalding stepped to the side to avoid the attack and caught a glimpse of red curly hair in the audience. Irene. She was watching.

A force slammed into Spalding's lower rib. It was a weak blow and easy to recover from. But the attack was enough to throw him off-guard, and he backed up slightly.

The crowd cheered and clapped. Some booed. Rightfully so; that was a foolish mistake.

Stay in the game, Spalding thought while shifting to face Michael. *This kid got a lucky blow.* Spalding had let his guard down because of a pretty face. Foolish. *Finish this, then I can ogle.*

Spalding stepped forward and took a swing, missing. He swung his leg right after, distracting Michael, then threw his second fist, this one grazing across his opponent's forearms and hitting him in the chest.

The crowd cheered and clapped as Spalding made another attack.

Michael dodged it and rolled onto the ground, getting back up onto his feet and facing his opponent.

Spalding turned to him and smirked. He liked the ambition of the kid. He apparently wanted to make something of himself. A part of Spalding wanted to spend more time with the lad and show him a few tricks. But with Irene watching, the stakes were a little higher than usual, and he couldn't lose this one.

He charged the kid again and stopped just before he got too close. The false attack psyched Michael out, and he dodged thin air, lowering his defences.

Spalding lunged his leg forward, knocking the young man in the calf and throwing him off-balance. He sent an uppercut to Michael's face, and it landed on his jaw. Spit and blood soared out of Michael's mouth as he flew into the air and fell flat on his back, knocked out.

The crowd roared with laughter and cheers. The fight was done; Spalding was the victor.

Spalding walked over to Michael and tapped his head with his foot. "Oi, you're not out, now, are you?"

Michael didn't reply. The kid had bitten off more than he could chew. It wasn't Spalding's fault that he was young and stupid.

Spalding rolled down his sleeves and took his jacket and hat. He'd have a break, maybe chat with Irene. Spalding exited the ring, squeezing through the crowd as some of the folks patted his arm and shoulder. He spotted the redhead on the outside of the ring. Spalding walked over to her with swagger in his step, like an ape winning dominance of the tribe.

"Saw you creeping in the back. Planning on recruiting me?" Spalding said.

Irene smiled and looked to the ground. "That poor boy had no chance against you."

"I warned him," Spalding shrugged. "Angsty young lad."

"Apparently." Irene folded her arms. "So, you're just here to throw a bunch of punches at inexperienced boys all night?"

"Is recruitment all you do all night?" Spalding said.

"It doesn't have to be."

That's what I want to hear, Spalding thought. "Then how about we get out of here?"

"Where?" Irene asked.

"Rowley is quite close; we're on the outskirts, really. There's a hotel."

Niles stepped towards the two of them, saying, "We should hit the road. This place is a waste of our time."

Irene looked over at him with a deathly gaze. "Leave, then. I'm staying."

Niles looked over at Spalding then over at her. "You really don't want to do this," he said to Irene.

"No, and you shouldn't have had that affair. Maybe we wouldn't be in this mess."

Niles pressed his lips together and folded his arms. He stared at Irene for several moments before sighing. "Fine. I suppose I owe you one, don't I?"

"For keeping your dirty little secret with the Black Hand?" Irene asked. "Yes. I think you do."

Black Hand affair? Spalding thought. Apparently mixing business and pleasure was taboo.

Irene patted Niles on the chest. "Don't squeal to my daddy."

Niles looked over at Spalding and pointed. "Watch yourself."

"Of course," Spalding said as Niles stormed off.

Spalding knew this was crazy. This was the daughter of Bran. Niles had just warned him too. Spalding knew better.

A gentle, small arm coiled around his own, fondling his biceps until the hands reached his shoulder. The arm hooked him into the gal's grasp. "Where were we?" Irene said in a honeyed voice.

"About to leave, if I recall?" Spalding said, looking down at her.

She pressed herself against his body, saying softly, "Take me, then."

That was it. Spalding's fate was sealed.

CHAPTER 10: Rumble Reward

CHAPTER 11

MATCH MET

Skin. Sweat. Panting. Moaning. That thing with the belt and tongue, what was that? Ending: bliss. This was not the typical night of passion Spalding was used to. This was something different. The lady of the evening had introduced him to a few new tricks and methods—all of them alluring.

Women. Their taste, their charm, their bodies. Traits that were all alluring. Women felt good for a while. The 'honeymoon phase,' as people say. After that the magic began to dwindle, then there wasn't much of anything left. He had experienced the wave of feelings over and over again with each woman he had been with. Spalding had been with enough that it seemed odd that he wasn't able to find one that would be considered suitable to be his wife. Who knew? Maybe they were all the same.

Maybe not.

The naked dimpled girl that lay next to him was rattling up something he hadn't felt before. She was different. The gal was also the first he had slept with that seemed to have more going on in her life. She was a businesswoman who showed she wanted to do more than be a housewife. His fascination with her was reinforced by the fantastic ass she had.

The sheets moved and the warm body beside him rolled away, leaving only a fading heat. A ghost of what had once been there. Spalding's eyes were still closed. The gunk in his eyes was thick, acting like glue that kept the lids shut. He stayed laying down,

presuming she'd return. Laying in a strange bed with a strange girl was an unmatched relaxation. It made the regular life of death and complications fizzle away.

The ruffling of clothes filled the silent space in the room. Then the sound of buckles and a zipper. Wait, was the girl leaving?

Spalding opened his eyes and sat up. His eyesight took a few moments to focus until he could clearly see Irene's butt in front of him as she pulled up her panties.

"Leaving so soon?" Spalding asked as he sat upright, still naked.

Irene didn't look back at him and continued to dress up. "Yes."

Spalding rubbed his chin. "Seems pretty abrupt considering the night we just shared." The words were honest, unprocessed, and genuine. There was something to her that kept drawing him in. He felt like a foolish kid who had his first crush on a girl.

Irene gave a devilish smile. "The type of night that we shared?"

"Yeah, here, naked in the bed."

"Oh, yes, that. It was a good brush last night, but I can't help you with your Irish toothache now. I'm quite late and need to get back to Chicago." Irene pulled up her trousers and buttoned up her blouse.

Spalding got up from the bed and walked over to Irene, casually sliding his hands onto her waist. "How about one more go before the road?"

Irene sighed and stepped out of his grasp. "I can't. The Black Hand are cutting into our operations. I'm needed."

Spalding snagged his trousers and shirt from the ground. "Alright, I get it. Can I buy you some breakfast before you go?"

Irene shook her head. "Not a chance. Cute offer, though."

Cute? That was something that Spalding hadn't heard in a while. He was much older now and, in a way, found the statement insulting.

Irene finished dressing and glanced back at him as she walked to the door. "Catch you around."

"That's it?" Spalding said, buttoning up his shirt. "No farewell kiss from the lady?"

"Nah, no such luck," Irene said. "Have a safe trip." She pulled open the door to the room and stormed off.

"Hey!" Spalding called out. Her footsteps muffled in the hall and faded away, leaving him alone.

Who does she think she is? Spalding had never experienced that kind of behaviour from a woman before. She clearly enjoyed sleeping with him. He felt her enjoy it and knew the difference between a woman faking and one genuinely enjoying the brush. Why was she so quick to leave?

Spalding couldn't help but smirk as he finished getting dressed. In a strange turn of events, Irene had behaved as Spalding had done before. She flew the coop as soon as she was able, so she didn't have to experience intimacy with him. He did it all the time with women. After a good time in the sack, you get the hell out of there as soon as you can. That way, they didn't get attached to you.

He gathered his things, paid for the hotel stay, exited, got his horse, and trotted out of Rowley. The sun had barely risen past the horizon, and most of the people were still asleep.

Irene, Spalding thought. He couldn't get her out of his mind as his horse trotted down the road leading out of town. He would return to Rutherford Manor, discuss business with Alastor, and see what their next snatch would be. The way back home always gave him plenty of time to let his mind wander.

The conversation between Niles and Irene entered his mind. Irene kept a dirty secret for Niles. Apparently, the two mobs were not supposed to ever mix. That seemed a bit old-fashioned, but it wasn't really any of Spalding's business. Then again, Niles had a Black Hand dead lover.

That family, Spalding thought, thinking about that night he and Alastor brutally murdered Donnie and his wife. Niles's lover died in the summer too. Were they one and the same? The kid, he got away with only a scar on his face. Did that kid tell the Black Hand about who murdered his family? If he did, they probably would have had a visit by now. Niles couldn't have seen the body. They would have heard about it, right? From Irene's words, it sounded like the White Hand were taking the heat for their mistake. It was all speculation and worries. The exact same concerns Spalding had shared with Alastor the night of the snatch, and nothing came of it.

Spalding journeyed down the forest road, just as he did on every trot back and forth from Rowley. He usually didn't pay much attention to the nature scenery. He mostly kept an eye out for anything unusual, like an animal, traps, or robbers creeping in the bush.

A group of four men on horses trotted along on the opposite side of the road. Spalding tightened the grip on his horse's strap. The group had feathers in their hair and animal hides wrapped around their shoulders. A couple carried bows; a few had rifles.

One of the nearby tribes, Spalding thought. They had to be coming back from a hunt.

The group of men crossed by Spalding and eyed him without blinking. Their horse saddles had no goods on them. Maybe they hadn't gone for a hunt. As long as they weren't looking for trouble, then it was of no concern to Spalding.

"Morning," Spalding said as they passed.

"Good day," said one of them. The others nodded back in a friendly manner and continued on their way.

Good, Spalding thought. He didn't want any issues while he was heading back from a night of fighting and passion. All he needed was to get back, bathe, and see if Alastor had any ideas on what they would do for their next snatch.

Another snatch. Irene, Spalding thought. Delivering another body to the White Hand meant they might run into Irene again. The girl who had turned the tables on Spalding.

Spalding continued down on the straight path until it took a curve, leading beyond a large tree. Past the trunk, a large furry mass was in the center of the road beside a smaller humanoid shape—a man.

What do we have here? Spalding thought while slowing his horse's pace.

The bear was sprawled out on the snowy road, and so was the man. They were both motionless. This could have been a draw. Spalding cautiously approached the scene, getting gradually closer until the man's characteristics came into view: black ponytail, burly form. Billy?

There was a decent amount of blood on the ground. It was impossible to tell whose blood it was. The only thing that was certain was that the fight had been messy. The bear's eyes were closed and it didn't appear to be breathing.

A groan came from the man and a sputter. He faced the snow below and attempted to look up. His movements were shaky, but he managed to lift his head up and stare at his new visitor.

It was Billy.

Spalding dismounted from his horse and leaned down beside him. He looked over at the bear and then over at Billy. "So, you didn't want to have a brawl with me, but you're crazy enough to go fight a bear?"

Billy's glazed-over eyes stared at him, or through—it was hard to tell. He let out a weak chuckle and shook his head.

"It appears you met your match, you crazy fool," Spalding said. "Are you bleeding?" he asked.

Billy let out a roar as he pushed himself up and rolled over onto his back, his one red-stained hand clutching his snow-sprinkled gut. "A scratch," Billy said.

"That is more than a scratch, but you'll survive." Spalding looked over to the road that he came from. "Did those men ambush you?"

"No," Billy said.

"Are they part of your tribe?"

"No, not anymore," Billy said as he tried to get up.

"How so?" Spalding asked. He scooched over and helped the man sit upright.

Billy panted. "They banished me. Well, the chief, my father, did and they simply made sure I left the tribe."

"What's with the bear then?"

"Bad luck, really. Perhaps the spirits have a cruel sense of humour, or they want me dead."

"I would be interested in hearing more about that," Spalding said. He stood up and extended his hand. "But first we need to get you some medical attention."

Billy stared at his hand. "I don't have any funds to visit your doctors."

"Nor do I, but I have some connections back at my manor." *Lilith*, Spalding thought. He knew the girl was good with her plants and could cook up some weird remedy to help Billy.

"I'll be fine. Thank you, though."

"I insist. You are hurt. You have no ride and are left in the cold. You were already foolish enough to fight a bear. Dare you chance it twice?"

Billy sighed. "Alright." He took Spalding's hand, and Spalding pulled on him. Billy had a lot more weight than Spalding had expected. Together, with groans, they got Billy onto his two feet. Both men were breathing heavily.

"Why are you helping me?" Billy asked.

"Because you are in need. I'm not going to leave someone out here to die; it'd be bad on my conscious." *Killing families and eating people isn't, though,* Spalding thought. It was a lie because those things did wear on him, but he had to have a sense of humour. Taking some amusement in the cruel acts was the only way he could stay sane.

Billy bowed his head. "You aren't like most men. I am humbled by your generosity."

"Please, don't be. I'd like to think any man would do the same for me."

"Unlikely. Men would probably rob you and leave you for dead," Billy said.

"True, and I didn't want that to happen to you." Spalding walked over to the horse and mounted.

Billy sauntered over to the animal. Spalding extended his hand and got the wounded man onto the horse. Billy wobbled and grunted, but he managed to make it up. He kept his arms around Spalding, so he didn't fall off.

"Let's get the hell out of here," Spalding said. "Hiya!"

The animal whimpered from the extra weight but continued onward. The horse trotted hastily through the forest, reaching the outskirts, and entered the snowy grass fields. From there, the path wasn't too far off from Rutherford Manor.

"So, you were at the fight club last night?" Spalding asked.

"Yes," Billy said.

"Were you banished last night from the tribe?"

"I had my suspicions; that is why I was in a hurry to leave. I had to talk to my father."

"Why go to the fight club if you were concerned about your father banishing you?"

"I was angry; I wanted to let my frustration out. But then I knew I shouldn't. The fight club is part of the problem. I. . . ." Billy paused. "I have an addiction."

"Don't we all?" *Women.*

"Not like this. I crave violence. It is a blood-curse in my family. I can't resist it, and my father knows." Billy coughed. "It is a long-winded story. How about I talk more when I am better?"

"Fair enough," Spalding said.

He wanted to know why the man had been banished by his father. What type of violent addiction could he have that was so dishonourable to even his own father? It would have to be something pretty dark. Possibly within the likes of what the Fleshers and Savidges did. Maybe Spalding could introduce Billy to his new family.

CHAPTER 12

LONG-TERM PLANNING

A cold steel table supported a body. Some blood drizzled onto the surface. Organs dangled out of the open gut of the corpse. Lanterns were mounted on both sides of the dead body, casting a soft light, allowing a clear view of the form. The yellow tint from the lanterns discoloured the corpse. This annoyed Nox. Unfortunately, the basement of Rutherford Manor had no natural light, and this was the best he had to work with.

His hands gently gripped an ink-dipped quill as he eyed the opened-up corpse in front of him. He guided his hand on the sheet of paper that rested on a wooden board against his knee. He copied every vein and every shape that he saw on the table. The stillness of a corpse was always comforting. Why couldn't people be more like them? Quiet and respectful.

Nox had only been working on human bodies since the summer and was still keen on documenting everything he could. It wasn't like they could afford one of those beautiful cameras, so he had to rely on his drawing skills to transfer them to immortality. The illustrations weren't perfect, but they were passable for his studies. Maybe if he had some paint colours, he could further render detail in the drawings.

Nox had learned to focus on his drawing from a young age when he started with animal corpses. He was obsessed with leaving a documented trail of everything he worked on. That skill had come in handy when he went to school. Now, he could use it to reference body parts for his future self's interest.

A knock came from the entrance hall leading back to the main level.

Nox looked up to see that Lilith was standing against the wood frame of the entryway. "Lilith, hello," he said as he continued to sketch.

Lilith smiled as she walked towards him. "Hello, dear, looks like you've been busy with this one," she said.

"Th-th-thank you. Father and Spalding picked him up yesterday. This is the third one I've worked with, and I have taken more care on the dissection."

"And the presentation of the organs." Lilith stood beside the operating table, eyeing the body. She also stood in front of his light. Now he couldn't draw. If it were anyone else, he would have been frustrated by the sudden interruption. Lilith was different, though. She cared for him, and she was the only one he felt a burning feeling for inside his heart. As far as he understood, that was the feeling of love. It was also the feeling of heartburn. Maybe that was all it was.

"Th-these human bodies are very fascinating," Nox said,

putting the paper and quill down.

"How so?" Lilith asked, walking over to him. She gently glided her hand against his chest and gave him a hug from behind.

"Humans are complicated. L-l-lots of parts compact inside of our skin. I have been experimenting with the solution we made in the summer. It has improved; it's more suitable for humans. It should make Father's job easier."

"Wonderful news." Lilith gently stroked his chest. "Nox, I feel something is out of the ordinary."

Nox looked up at her. She stared into his eyes with a gaze of care and acceptance. She never did stare at the scars on his face. Lilith was a rare soul. She really could look past people's physique. He admired that about her.

"What do you mean?" Nox asked.

"Something is lingering in the air. You know that feeling I had when the accident happened?"

"Y-y-yes. You had it the whole day," Nox said.

"It's that same feeling. That unsettling rot of something just behind my heart." She let go of him and pressed on her forehead. "I can't really explain it."

Nox pressed his lips together. She brought up her feelings semi-frequently, as if she were attuned to another sense. He wasn't sure if it was made up in her head or if there was truth to it. There had been truth to her insight into the explosion. Then again, if you claim you have enough otherworldly feelings, eventually one of them is going to land true. It was a simple process of stubbornness to success.

"I'm not sure. I just wanted to come down and see you," Lilith said, her voice trembling. "The last time I had this feeling, something bad happened to you."

Nox put his illustrative tools down and got up from his chair, taking her hands. "N-n-nothing bad is going to happen. I am here. P-p-please do not worry."

Lilith smiled at him. "I'll try not to. These emotions, these feelings I get are impossible to express with words. They're complex, like an abstract painting. There is depth, layers, and they come and go as I meet certain people or see particular signs. I'm not sure if that makes any sense."

Nox gave her hands a squeeze and let go. "I'm afraid that I don't fully understand. I believe you, though."

That was partially true. Nox had a difficult time understanding her supernatural claims. He was a believer in science. Everything could be explained with reason, and the things that have yet to be solved could and would be as science evolved. The number zero used to cause chaos. The suggestion of the world being a spherical shape once struck fear into the hearts of ordinary folk. Now, people accept these things as part of their daily lives. Lilith's odd feelings could just be another case of unexplained science.

Lilith fell forward, wrapping her arms around Nox and closing her eyes. "Thank you," she said while hugging him tightly.

Nox gently stroked her hair, embracing her for a few moments before urging her to let go. He wanted to get back to his illustration before the corpse began to decay.

"Nox." Lilith stroked her hair. "This may seem a bit sudden, but we've been together for a while now."

"Yes," Nox said.

"What are we going to do?"

"I don't follow?"

"Well, you will eventually become head of the household, following in the footsteps of your father," Lilith said.

"He'll get married," came a booming voice from the hallway.

Lilith and Nox looked over to see a towering being walk into the light. His long grey hair swayed side to side as he entered. Alastor.

Lilith took a curtsy. "Mr. Flesher."

"F-f-father, what can I do for you?" Nox asked.

"I came for some of the solution," Alastor said.

"You're not snatching today, are you?" Nox asked.

"No, but I want to have some extra on hand," Alastor said. "I need to go into town, but that is now secondary to my visit. Forgive my intrusion, but this discussion caught my interest."

"N-n-not at all, Father. Please, continue," Nox said.

"Eventually, Nox," Alastor started, "you are going to take over the household, and you will need a strong, lovely lady by your side. Trust me, your wife will be your backbone. I know Matilda was mine." Alastor eyed Lilith.

Nox and Lilith exchanged looks. She had a warm, closed smile, and Nox was expressionless, as he always was.

"I would be honoured," Lilith said.

"M-m-marriage?" Nox asked. He thought about the question for a moment. It wasn't out of the picture. Marriage made sense because it was the next natural progression of his life: carry on the family name. He also felt deeply for Lilith and would not want her to leave him. This would be a logical choice.

"I would like that," Nox said.

Alastor smiled. "That sounds wonderful. You might need to

propose to the young lady, son."

Nox looked at his father and scratched his head. He wanted to initiate but realized he wasn't prepared. "I-I-I don't have a ring."

"I don't care!" Lilith said.

Here I go. Nox remained motionless for several moments. Does one just kneel and propose? He wasn't sure. But apparently, this was what was going to happen. Untraditional. Nox got down on one knee and took Lilith's hand. His voice stuttered, but not from his condition. This was because of his heart. He pushed through the sudden burst of nervousness and spoke, every vowel vibrating against his ribcage. He felt each word. "L-l-lilith Blum, will you marry me?"

Lilith gripped his hand tightly. "Yes! Nox, yes, I will!"

CHAPTER 13

OUTCASTS

The horse wheezed and panted as it trotted along the frozen road. The poor animal was getting some thorough training that neither its owner or the animal expected it to receive. This was not the horse's usual routine. Whether it was aware of its role or not, it was acting as a life-saving transport device. Spalding believed he had a heart and couldn't possibly leave Billy to die on the side of the road. That would be inhumane.

They reached Rutherford Manor, and the horse came to a stop. Now that poor animal could finally have a rest.

"Good job, gal," Spalding said while hopping off the animal. "You ready?" he asked Billy as he extended his hands.

Billy groaned and slid off the horse on his own. "Feeling woozy," he said.

"Aye, put your arm around me," Spalding said, grabbing the man's arm and placing it over his shoulders. He helped the man walk as Billy clutched his gut. The bleeding hadn't stopped, and it had smeared over the horse's saddle. It was time to take care of the wound.

The two men hobbled up onto the veranda and to the entrance. Spalding pulled out his keys and unlocked the front door, swinging it open wildly. He stomped into the foyer, hoping that someone inside would hear him.

"Hello!" Spalding called out. The manor was large and still relatively empty, but someone should be here.

Footsteps creaked as Vivian appeared around the corner from the living room, holding her doll. "Spalding! You're back." She looked at Billy and then her doll. "Look, he brought a visitor."

"Vivian, can you fetch Lilith? We need to tend to this man's wounds," Spalding said.

"Of course. They're in the basement," Vivian said. She dashed around the corner, through the hall, and down to the second level.

"We'll get you some help," Spalding said to Billy.

"Thank you, again," he said.

Within a few moments, Vivian re-appeared at the entrance, this time bringing Alastor, Nox, and Lilith with her.

"My god," Alastor said, looking at Billy's wounds.

"Yeah, he is a little worse for wear. Lilith, can you help him?"

Lilith held her hands to her lips, staring at Billy's open wound. "I believe so." She looked at Nox, then back at Billy.

Nox nodded. "Th-th-there should be something we can do."

"Excellent. Where should we take him?" Spalding asked.

"Here, with me," Lilith said. "Probably best not to do stairs?"

"No," Billy said weakly.

Spalding and Billy followed Lilith through the hall and to the kitchen table. It was no operating table, but it would have to do.

Lilith hurried to clear the table of a few items and took them into the kitchen. Alastor appeared with a blanket and spread it over the table.

"Alright, let's get you to lie down," Spalding said as he let go of Billy.

Billy sat on the table and lay himself down as Lilith arrived back on the scene with some jars filled with ointments, a cloth, and a medical kit.

Alastor gently put his arm around Spalding, guiding him into the hallway. "Spalding, walk with me." He led Spalding out of the entryway and outside onto the veranda. "Who is that man?" he asked.

"Billy comes to the fight club on a regular basis," Spalding said.

"Why is he here?"

"I found him on the side of a road. The fool took on a bear and got himself injured. He would have frozen to death if I didn't bring him back."

"Why not take him to a doctor?"

"It's not like I have any cash to afford that."

"Doesn't he?"

Spalding folded his arms. "He also doesn't have a place to stay anymore. His tribe banished him."

Alastor nodded. "He has nowhere else to go."

"That's correct," Spalding said. "I was thinking on the ride here that he might be of use. The manor has been quiet lately, and he would make a good addition to supporting everyone."

"What makes you think he wants to stay?" Alastor asked.

"I've got a hunch. Billy has nothing else, and he has a tendency to want to inflict violence. Something not too unfamiliar to our own past."

Alastor nodded. "That is true. So, he's an outsider."

"Yes."

"We're all outsiders at Rutherford Manor in some form or another. This is the place that we call home. See if he is interested and if he is, he can stay."

"Perfect," Spalding said.

Alastor patted him on the back. "Now, you must excuse me. I was about to head into town."

"Rowley?" Spalding asked.

"No, Chicago."

"What are you going to make that hike for?" Spalding asked.

"Bran wanted to meet and discuss our operations."

"What about? Think that second snatch has caught up to us? Niles and Irene told me the Black Hand is causing them some trouble."

"Of course; they are rivals."

"It involved Donnie's death," Spalding said.

"I don't think that is the case. I'm beginning to wonder if Bran suspects how we continually obtain such freshly deceased. They're mobsters, not murderers. I'll fill you in when I get back."

"Why don't I join you? Sounds like it could be a tricky conversation. I could offer some backup for our case."

Alastor shook his head. "No, you have your hands quite full enough here. Focus on our guest at the moment; he is going to need some attention. Like I said, I will fill you in when I return."

"Okay. Be on the cautious side."

"Always."

"Swift travels," Spalding said.

"Thank you, Spalding. As I've said before, you'd make your father proud." Alastor nodded and stepped down the stairs, walking over to their stables where they housed the animals. He reached the gate and shooed a grey owl that rested on the door before opening it, and then disappeared into the stables.

Spalding would have preferred to have gone with Alastor to see why Bran wanted to contact him. Was it an excuse to talk about Donnie's death? Bran was a straight shooter and said what was on his mind. Whatever the case was, it was going to be a tough meeting and Spalding wanted to back up his partner. Then again, Spalding did need to attend to their new guest. Billy needed attention, and Spalding had been the one who brought him here.

Alastor burst out of the stables on horseback and stormed onto the road, waving goodbye. Spalding returned the gesture before going inside. Billy's grunts were audible from the dining room. At least the man was still alive.

"There!" Lilith said while stepping back from Billy. The man lay flat on the dining-room table with his shirt off. Lilith had a bucket of water, a blood-stained cloth, and her tools spread out on the table. Nox was gone, probably back in his study. The boy was never much for comforting newcomers.

"Don't touch the paste. Let it soak into your skin and let the stitches do the rest," Lilith said.

"What is it?" Billy asked.

"It's a homemade remedy. Primarily yarrow and goldenrod,"

Lilith said.

"Impressive, you know nature well," Billy said.

Spalding stepped forward. "She is a brilliant mind. We're lucky to have her," he said.

Lilith blushed as she began to organize her things. "You're all too kind. Thank you."

"See, Billy?" Spalding said. "Told you we'd get you patched up."

"Thank you, Spalding. I am forever in your debt."

Spalding walked around and sat down on one of the chairs, so he could be closer to Billy's eye level.

"Tell me, Billy, what happened with you and your father? What did you do that was so horrible for him to banish you?" Spalding felt like he was prying a bit much. The man was wounded, but he had to know who he really was. They'd had a few discussions at the fight club, but he really didn't know much about Billy. He was pretty much a stranger in their home.

Billy sighed. "Do you really want to know?"

"I do."

Lilith got a handful of her items and hurried out of the room, leaving the bucket of bloody water and the cloth.

"This dates back before me. My mother was emotionally unstable, sick, and desperate to have a child. The spirits were not kind to my mother and father, and they could not conceive."

"Unfortunate," Spalding said.

"It was. This is what drove my mother to insanity. She begged the spirits, but they did not answer her. She resorted to dark arts, seeking high and low for anyone or *anything* that would listen." Billy grunted as he sat up, resting on one arm. He looked at Spalding. "Something did answer."

Spalding crossed his legs and leaned back. He had heard plenty of spook stories in his days. Spalding personally felt that the most horrific things were done by people to people. However, he was willing to buy into what Billy had to share.

"The something," Billy continued, "was not of the spirit world. What she contacted was of another plane. Muunat, a shapeshifting demon of unfathomable powers. My mother made the first contact with the demon and begged her to give her a child. The demon Muunat was willing to grant her wish, but she would have to sacrifice her soul to give birth to another life. My mother, she sacrificed herself for my existence."

"She died during your birth?" Spalding asked.

"She survived the pregnancy. Not long after, she died in her sleep. My father was devastated. I was young, very young. Her death showed no signs of disease or murder, but her face was a ghostly white, and her flesh sucked dry. Something otherworldly took place during her slumber and drained her soul from this plane."

"Alright, what does that have to do with you?" Spalding asked.

"Have you ever encountered a demon, Spalding?"

"Does in bed count?" Spalding grinned.

Billy didn't smile.

Spalding wiped his face. "Can't say I have, no."

"Demons are full of trickery. They say they will offer you something but never explain the full agreement. Demons use clever words that attack the weak-hearted. When Muunat blessed my mother with the gift of birth, she also cursed the offspring."

"You?"

"Yes, Muunat cursed the offspring with her desire for destruction. The demon is always working in the shadows, watching, orchestrating chaos, violence, and misery. I was born with that trait."

Spalding uncrossed his legs and leaned forward. "You're telling me you're part demon?"

"No, I don't believe so. Demons affect the soul. My soul is tainted with evil, and I cannot control my addiction."

Lilith returned to the room. She smiled at both of them as she gathered the bucket and cloth. "Don't mind me," she said. "I'll be out of your hair momentarily." She hurried out of the room with the bucket, the echoes of her footsteps fading through the house.

Spalding raised his arms. "That's it?"

"Yes." Billy squinted. "You don't seem ill at ease."

"No," Spalding smirked. "That isn't that bad."

"What do you mean?"

"Demons, ghosts, spirits. That isn't out of the ordinary here. Believe me, we've been through it all, if not worse, to try and get out of poverty."

"I see. This household is for those with tainted souls."

"Something like that. Yeah." Spalding cleared his throat. "On that note, I have to ask . . . do you have any plans now that your tribe gave you the boot?"

"I have yet to think that far ahead," Billy said. "This has all happened so fast."

"Alastor and I had a bit of a chat. We're more than willing to let you stay."

Billy nodded. "I am in your debt, and you have shown me a level of kindness that I am unfamiliar with. I am afraid, though. What of my addictions? I don't want to hurt you or your family."

"I've got a solution: How about we keep going to the fight club?"

"I would like that," Billy said with a smile.

"Welcome to the family."

CHAPTER 14

HEADMASTER

Two days passed. Two days sweating away in the basement of Rutherford Manor. It was difficult to know the exact amount of time that had gone by considering there was no light. The only sense of time Nox had was when Lilith came down to check on him. Her arrivals seemed to be evenly spread across when meal times were, and bedtime. Nox had a reliable internal clock. It was partly why he was efficient at managing all of the projects he had on the go.

Dissections, contraptions, chemical and biological experimentations, you name it. Nox was working on all types of projects. The biggest distraction was that both Vivian and Spalding came down on a couple of occasions to inform him that his father had not returned from his trip to Chicago. That worried Nox. Worry interfered with his thought process and resulted in slow progress.

Nox carefully took his screwdriver to a screw bolted upon a

gear in place for a metallic contraption that formed the basic shape of a hand. Half of it was encased with metal and the second half of the shell was left on the table. With this layout, he could gain access to all of the internal moving parts. Just another experimentation of his.

Imagine if human limbs could be replaced with metal ones. A crazy thought. It would also be a fantastic achievement. The plan was simple: finish the arm and apply it to the next body that Father and Spalding provided him. As long as there weren't any distractions, Nox knew he could pull it off.

"Nox," came a raspy voice from the hallway.

Nox's screwdriver slipped and missed the unscrewed gear, sending it tumbling into the innards of the hand. "Dammit!" Nox hissed. "What?"

Spalding raised an eyebrow at Nox. "I hope I didn't interrupt you."

"N-n-no, apologies. This is just tedious work." Nox turned around in his swivel chair to face him. "Yes?"

"The sheriff is here," Spalding said.

"And?"

"He has something to share with us. Please come upstairs with Vivian and I."

Nox really didn't want to leave, but he had to. Was this related to his father? Possibly. Regardless, now he had a more significant interruption to finishing the mechanical arm. He picked up the lamp from his desk, extinguished the second one, and followed Spalding out of the basement. Reaching ground level, he blew out the light of his lantern and entered the foyer. Sheriff Jenson stood by the doorway. Vivian was only a few feet away, hugging Lilith.

"Vivian? Lilith" Nox asked, eyeing the pink-faced girls. Tears drizzled down their cheeks. He saw his sister cry on a semi-regular basis when she argued with her toy, but never Lilith.

Sheriff Jenson had his hands on his belt, pushing back his long coat with the golden sheriff badge. "This Alastor's boy?" the sheriff asked. He didn't seem phased by Nox's face. He had to be used to mangled bodies with his job.

"Aye," Spalding said while placing a hand on Nox's shoulder. Spalding never did that. Why would he put his hand on Nox? Physical touch was not Spalding's language, at least with him.

"We have unfortunate news about your father," the sheriff said.

"What do you mean?" Nox asked.

The sheriff looked at Spalding then at Nox. "We found Alastor's body on the side of the road early this morning."

"What?" Nox felt his heart sink. Was this a dream? Or a cruel prank? The words that the sheriff spoke didn't seem to be real. "Wh-wh-where is he?"

Spalding squeezed his shoulder. "We'd like to see the body, to confirm," he said.

"We can do that," the sheriff said. "We found Mr. Flesher on his way to Chicago, shortly after the split-off to Rowley. I'd guess he had been there for about two days based on the frost on his skin."

"How?" Vivian whaled.

"We don't know yet; we just found the body," the sheriff said. "Do you know where he was going?"

"To Chicago, to my knowledge," Spalding said.

"What for?" Sheriff Jenson asked.

"We do business there frequently," Spalding said.

"What kind?" Sheriff Jenson said.

"We connect people."

"As in?"

"We see people with suitable traits and link them with potential jobs. We take a cut from the companies," Spalding said.

"I see," Sheriff Jenson said.

Vivian peeked up, saying, "Can you take us to him?"

"It is a bit of a hike from here," said Sheriff Jenson.

"That's fine," Spalding said. "We'll prepare the carriage."

It felt surreal. Between the words of Sheriff Jenson, Spalding's calm and controlled behaviour, and the crying of Lilian and Vivian, none of it was normal. This was not how life was supposed to go. Nox's father had yet to show him any of the inner workings of their family's business. This couldn't be real. Nox could not accept his father's demise until he saw him for himself.

Spalding and their new house member, Billy, gathered the horse and clipped it to the carriage. Billy stayed to watch the manor while Lilith, Vivian, Spalding, and Nox gathered in the wagon. Their ride was quiet, minus the sniffling and crying of the girls. Nox was still in disbelief. He couldn't accept it. What would that mean if his father was dead? Nox would have to take care of the Flesher family name. It wasn't like he could rely on his brother, Walter.

The carriage followed the sheriff's horse, trotting to the crime scene where blue-and-white coloured rope was set up with posts to block off a body lying face-down on the side of the road. The deputy stood by the body and waved at the newcomers.

"Shit," Spalding muttered.

Nox looked up at him, then back to the body. Could that really be his father?

The carriage stopped, and the family piled out to the crime scene.

"Stay behind the rope, please," Sheriff Jenson said.

Nox leaned over the rope to get a closer look of the tall, wide-framed body. The black peacoat, thin grey hair, and brown slacks were characteristic of his father. Alastor Flesher was dead. Nox's heart was punched inward by an invisible force, and his stomach began to fold in on itself. He was ready to puke.

Vivian howled in the loss and fell into Nox's shoulder. He lost his balance momentarily before getting a firm grip on her. Her tears were toxic, and he began to experience some of his own drizzling out from his eyelids. His lips trembled as his nose began to drip. This was real emotion.

This can't be happening, Nox thought as his mind ran simulated scenarios through his head. Managing the money, his marriage with Lilith, being a caring husband, working with Spalding directly, and maintaining the household of Rutherford Manor . . . all of this was now his responsibility. He was just a boy. He had a few years before he would even be considered a man. He hadn't graduated university. Life played a cruel trick on him and his goals.

"How long did you say he been here?" Spalding asked.

"Well, we're going to guess a couple of days," the deputy said, keeping his hands on his belt.

"No one saw him over the past forty-eight hours?' Spalding asked.

"Look," Sheriff Jenson said while extending his hand, "we're doing all that we can here. We need you folks to understand that. The coroner is going to come and investigate the body, but it doesn't look like any foul play. He has no inflicted wounds. Not even his clothes are torn."

"Where's his horse?" Spalding continued to nag. "None of this is making any sense."

Lilith shook her head and lifted the bottom of her dress as she ducked under the rope.

"Hey!" the deputy shouted. "Get out of there."

Spalding blocked the man from hopping over the rope. "Let her do what she needs to," Spalding said.

"She'll tamper with the evidence," the deputy argued.

"I won't," Lilith called back.

She got down onto her knees and extended her hand over Alastor's body. She waved it back and forth as she closed her eyes, breathing steadily.

That girl and her extra senses, Nox thought. Lilith was always a believer in the world that cannot be seen, only felt. Nox humoured her and didn't care at this point. Everything was upside down now.

"The hell she doin'?" the deputy asked.

Sheriff Jenson shook his head in disapproval. "I will never understand you Fleshers," he said.

"I'm a Savidge, thank you," Spalding corrected. "We all mourn in our own way. Please respect that."

Lilith opened her eyes. "He was murdered," she said.

The deputy snorted. "Excuse me, little lady, but leave the final decision-making to the experts. There's no sign of struggle here."

Lilith ignored him and leaned over beside Alastor's extended arm. His hand was clutched. She tugged on it lightly, but his hand was frozen. "He is gripping something," she said.

"Wh-what?" Nox asked.

"I, I, I can't really tell," Lilith said. "Maybe feathers?"

Spalding eyed the sheriff. "And there were no signs of struggle?"

"We saw that," Sheriff Jenson said. "It doesn't mean any confrontation was made. He might have shooed a bird."

"Th-th-that's a lie!" Nox shouted. The sudden shout caused everyone to go silent, realizing that the dead man's children were here, grieving.

Spalding walked over to Vivian and Nox and wrapped his arms around them. "We'll get through this." He looked up at Sheriff Jenson. "How long will the coroner be?"

"He only needs about a day," Sheriff Jenson said.

"We'd like to have a proper funeral," Spalding said.

"Of course," Sheriff Jenson said. "If you have any additional information about what Mr. Flesher was doing, let us know."

"We will," Spalding said. He squeezed Nox and Vivian before letting them go. "Stay strong, we will have time to mourn the great man that was your father."

"Daddy!" Vivian cried.

"Nox," Spalding said.

Nox looked up at him and wiped the tears from his face.

"Take care of your sister today. You and I will chat more about keeping your father's legacy alive later."

"Of c-c-course," Nox said. He didn't really know what else to say to Spalding. This was all so sudden. How did his father die? He was a strong man and had no enemies. Whatever the reason was, it was in the past. In the present, Nox was now the headmaster of the Fleshers.

ACT III

BARGAINING

CHAPTER 15

MESSENGER OF DEATH

What went wrong? One moment life was looking to be on the upswing for the folks of Rutherford Manor. They had real food and money. The Fleshers' future looked bright with Nox, and Spalding was, well, still himself—chasing beautiful women and killing people to survive. All of it was gone now. Now, Spalding would have to pick up the pieces that Alastor left behind in his disturbingly mysterious death. Everything was unfamiliar now.

The White Hand was Spalding's first thought when Sheriff Jenson showed up to their home. He couldn't think of anyone else that would want to have Alastor dead. The Fleshers were very careful about who and how they murdered.

Perhaps the White Hand had finally learned how Spalding and Alastor obtained the bodies. Or maybe Bran wasn't involved, and this had to do with the Black Hand. There was that Donnie character and his family that Alastor and Spalding had killed.

They needed answers, and the law was not on their side with this. They were in too deep in illegal activities. Spalding would have to investigate privately. The one ally—if you could call her one—that could offer insight was Irene. She seemed to walk her own path, and she did have dirt on Niles's affair. She didn't play by her dad's rules. That gal had her own agenda, whatever that was. Perhaps Spalding could arrange a meet up with her. He could see the girl's dimple again, maybe get her out of her clothes too.

Spalding first had to attend to the immediate tasks of taking care of Alastor's funeral. Lilith was willing to step in where Nox failed to: organizing the funeral. The boy was brilliant, but he was lacking in some key points of basic knowledge. Common courtesy was one. Business practice was another. The list could go on.

Thankfully, Spalding was not wholly alone. Billy had come to Rutherford Manor at the best time: the worst time. If the pair hadn't met a couple days ago, Spalding would be dealing with all this chaos on his own.

After the family received the news from the coroner, they were able to begin planning the funeral. The coroner didn't find anything suspicious in Alastor's death, just like the sheriff had said. Alastor's cold, clenched hand had gripped a few feathers. Nothing else.

The coroner summarized the death as a heart attack. Spalding thought it unlikely, if Lilith's reading was anything to go by. At least they were able to begin planning their grieving process. Now, the task was to inform those who cared for Alastor that they must say their final goodbyes.

Most of Alastor's loved ones were at Rutherford Manor. There were maybe a few in Rowley who Alastor had grown to be friendly with during church. Then there was the oldest Flesher son. It was up to Spalding to inform Walter of the news. He couldn't imagine Nox trying to get his brother to come to their father's funeral. The two didn't talk anymore.

Spalding's horse trotted along and the man kept his gaze forward while he travelled to Walter Flesher's home. The man hadn't moved too far away from Rowley. He had a farm, from the last Spalding had heard. Alastor had tried to get in contact with him several times before his death but his attempts only resulted in silence.

The path took Spalding to a farmstead where he spotted an automobile parked out front of the home. A tall, broad-shouldered man was kneeled down beside the car with tools, working away. It was Walter; he eerily resembled a younger copy of his father.

Walter was ghostly pale as he looked up to see Spalding approaching on horseback. There was a red-headed girl—had to be about sixteen—at the foyer of the home, standing to Walter's side. He got to his feet and tried to stand in front of her to hide her blood-covered hands.

Odd, Spalding thought. *That's a lot of blood on a kid.* It couldn't be the girl's blood. Seeing that at Rutherford Manor was normal. Seeing blood on the daughter of a Flesher who shunned the family line of activity was not. Maybe that was why Walter was so pale. Perhaps it was best not to ask.

Spalding brought his horse to a stop and hopped off of the

saddle. He tipped his hat at the two and pointed at the car. "Seems like you've been doing well. An automobile. I hear they're quite the experience."

Walter stood tall, moving in front of the small girl. "Good day, Spalding," he said. His voice was just as booming as his father's. "Last time we saw each other you were still a boy, eighteen years ago."

Spalding smirked. "As were you, if I recall." *Same age and he's got a family and house. Then you have me,* Spalding thought. The reflection of age and life comparison was another jab at Spalding's lack of marriage. He managed to shake it off. *Unimportant right now.*

"I'm not interested in small talk, Spalding. You know why I denied my father's attempts at contact and I don't need him sending you now."

"Don't worry, I have nothing to say to you either. I'm here to deliver your father's last message."

"I beg your pardon?" Walter asked.

"Alastor is dead," Spalding said. The words were so matter-of-fact, yet hard for him to grasp. "He would like you to say goodbye."

Walter blinked a couple of times. He cleared his throat. "I'm not going back to Rutherford Manor."

"We don't need you to. Nox is Alastor's successor. I am simply here to invite you to the funeral."

The girl peeked around her father, her wide hazelnut eyes staring at Spalding.

Spalding shifted his stance to leave, saying, "However, it looks like you're a bit preoccupied. Getting a taste of the old family ways?" He couldn't help himself; he had to throw a jab at Walter. The Flesher had left Rutherford Manor so dramatically, offended by his family's attempts to survive. Now, here he was with an oddly suspicious recreation of the past with his daughter.

The Fleshers just can't get away from death and blood, no matter how far they run away, Spalding thought.

Walter looked sheepishly down at his daughter's bloody hands. His faced curled into a scowl as he said, "You think I would introduce. . . . With my daughter? I am not Alastor!"

Spalding raised his arms. "The funeral is in exactly three days. Do as you want." He returned to his horse and mounted, leaving the eldest Flesher to deal with whatever mess he had. It wasn't Spalding's concern. The message had been delivered.

CHAPTER 16

FIRST COMMAND

Death. A cold fact that everyone is aware of and ultimately experiences in their lifetime. The act of passing has been one of the biggest mysteries to humankind. Where does one go when they die? The church would have you believe that you enter heaven when you leave this world, as long as you confessed your sins before you died. Otherwise, you'd burn in Hell. All religions have attempted to explain the unexplainable. Death was a mystery, and each person learns the truth on their own, when they die. For those that are left behind, they are to grieve, mourn, and celebrate the life that was once amongst them.

That selfish bastard, Spalding thought. He'd felt a pain inside of him when he first learned of Alastor's death; now, that sense of loss had evolved into a strange form of anger. Alastor's death was not an accident. The man was off to meet the White Hand the day he went missing. If Spalding had been there, would the events have played out differently? Would Alastor still be dead?

Why didn't he just let me join him? Spalding thought. *Secrets, he always had secrets. That's why he died.* Spalding hated thinking ill of his former business partner. He also hated how Alastor kept plans hidden, and surmised this had ultimately led to his demise.

Internal chatter—not really suitable for those around me, or the scene. Spalding cupped his hands tightly, resting them in front of him. He stared forward, along with the other four funeral attendees. The immediate family. Billy was to his left, Vivian to his right, Lilith after her, and Nox on the far end. No one else came to pay their respects for Alastor.

Spalding had forgotten how the folk of Rowley had grown distant from Alastor as the Fleshers became progressively poorer. Then the cannibalism happened. The people of the town didn't know, but they could sense something was different. It was true—once you eat human flesh, you don't see people the same.

The priest, Father Isaac, stood on the opposite side from the group, across the open black casket where Alastor lay. The perished Flesher's eyes were closed, his hands on his chest. The stress-induced gray hairs and wrinkles would no longer progress on Alastor's ageing face. The man was now at peace.

Father Isaac held his Bible, speaking loudly to be heard over the loud wind. "In the Name of God, the merciful Father, we commit the body of Alastor Flesher to the peace of the grave."

Sobbing and crying erupted from the group. It was probably one of the girls, Spalding thought; Nox tended to bottle up his emotions. Spalding looked over to see Vivian was stroking her doll like a madwoman. Her nose and eyes dripped onto the toy, making its face moist.

Spalding extended his arm and hugged the girl tightly. She didn't need some stupid doll; she needed human contact. Vivian reacted as expected, and wrapped her arms around him, squeezing him with force, sobbing into his coat.

"From dust you came," Father Isaac continued, "to dust you shall return. Jesus Christ, our Saviour, shall raise you up on the last day."

Unlikely. Nice words, though, Spalding thought.

"Would anyone like to say a few words about Mr. Flesher before we lay him to rest?" Father Isaac said.

Spalding thought about it. He wanted to, but couldn't think of anything nice to say at the moment. He'd just had to get mad at Alastor on the day of his funeral. If he got up in front of everyone, he'd surely insult the Fleshers.

"I d-d-do," Nox said as he stepped forward.

Father Isaac extended his hand as Nox stood beside him.

The group stood tall, giving attention to the new headmaster of Rutherford Manor.

"M-m-my father was a hardworking man. H-h-he housed every one of us that are here today. His heart was big and was accepting of everyone who didn't f-f-fit into the rest of the world. He knew us all well. He had personal relations with all of us that were unique to everyone." Nox paused, eyeing each person, fighting back the tears that pooled on his eyelids. "He was respected among his peers and also feared by them. He was a crafty businessman and m-m-made sure we always had something to eat and a roof over our heads. He was taken from us far too soon, and n-n-none of us were ready for it. I can't even begin to f-f-fathom filling in the shoes that he left. I-I-I want to carry on his legacy to the best of my abilities, to be as sm-sm-smart as him, strong and compassionate. I will honour him. Father, Alastor Flesher." Nox's voice trembled as he wiped his face.

"Thank you, Nox," Father Isaac said, gently patting him on the back.

He barely stuttered, Spalding thought as the boy walked around back to his spot with Lilith. The girl embraced him in her arms.

"Anyone else?" Father Isaac asked.

Not unless you want a series of curse words and foul statements, Spalding thought.

"Very well, we will leave the casket open for each of you to say your last goodbyes," Father Isaac said while stepping away.

"I am so sorry," Billy whispered to Spalding.

"Don't be; you arrived at an unfortunate time," Spalding said.

"I feel responsible."

Spalding squinted at him. "That's ludicrous. Why?"

"My curse. I can't think of anything else that would cause such a horrific thing."

"Nonsense, you barely knew Alastor or what type of troubles we got ourselves into. This runs deeper than your arrival."

Billy nodded. He didn't seem convinced. Spalding understood; the man seemed just as troubled as the company around him.

A mechanical sound and sputtering came from the distance, growing louder as an automobile rolled on up to the burial site. Not many folks had those mechanical beasts, but the eldest

Flesher son did. There were three people in the horseless buggy too, with the driver being a tall, wide-shouldered man. The car parked, and the engine turned off.

The funeral attendees looked over at the newcomers: a girl, a woman and a man, who exited the vehicle and slowly walked over to the burial site. They were dressed in black and huddled close to each other, walking with cautious steps.

Nox looked over at them, his face turning from a slanted gaze into a curled expression of fury within seconds.

"Looks like the ghost of the past came to pay respects," Spalding muttered. "Billy." Spalding nudged his head at Vivian. The man took the girl into his arms as she continued to weep.

Spalding adjusted his hat and hurried over to the newcomers. He figured it'd be better if he dealt with Walter and his family compared to Nox. Nox might say something stupid.

"Afternoon," Spalding said as he tipped his hat.

"Spalding," Walter said. His wife and daughter stood behind him. The teenager waved.

"Penny!" Walter said. "Lita, please."

The lady wrapped her arm around her daughter's shoulder, bringing her closer to the group. "We aren't going to interact with these people," the lady, identified as Lita, said.

"Why, Mom? They're family, right?" Penny asked.

Walter looked down at her. "No. We are never going to see them again."

"It is good to see you say goodbye," Spalding said. It seemed like the polite thing to say, even though he didn't care to tell it.

"We won't be making a grand appearance to everyone. We are just here to pay our respects, then we are leaving."

"I wouldn't expect anything else." Spalding stepped aside. "Please."

"Thank you," Walter said. The man and his family walked over to the open casket.

I'd best keep Nox occupied, Spalding thought. The less that the two brothers interacted, the simpler the funeral would be. "Nox," he said. "That was a beautiful speech."

"Th-th-thank you," Nox said. "I hope what I say, I can do. For the sake of everyone."

Lilith stroked his shoulder. "You will. I believe in you."

"We all do," Spalding said. *I'm just hoping.* The sad truth was that Spalding was so uncertain of Nox's ability. The boy was still young and had a lot to learn.

"I-I-I don't want my father's death to be in vain," Nox said. "We need answers. I want to find who did this."

"We all do. Now that we've paid our respects to Alastor, we'll get to the bottom of this."

"I sensed something," Lilith said. "When I was near him, by the side of the road."

"What do you mean?" Spalding asked.

"He was murdered. I could feel his agony, the fear he felt before his death. Those are not the type of feelings you get when you pass from natural causes."

"Th-th-think his work had anything to do with this?" Nox asked.

"Possibly," Spalding said. "His horse was missing. Perhaps they attacked him somewhere else and dumped him on the side of the road."

"But he didn't have any signs of struggle," Lilith said. "I think he was poisoned."

"Poisoned?" Spalding asked. "But the coroner mentioned no such thing."

"There are methods of untraceable poison," Lilith said.

"Wh-wh-where was my father going when he left?" Nox asked.

"He said he was going into Chicago to deal with the White Hand," Spalding said.

"Why didn't you go with him?" Nox asked.

"I ask myself the same question," Spalding said.

"D-did the White Hand have something against the body-snatching?" Nox asked.

"Not that I was aware of. Everything was going smoothly except for the day he left."

"Wh-what?" Nox asked.

"He said Bran, the boss, wanted to discuss our body-snatching process. Alastor had concerns if they were beginning to suspect we were simply killing people."

"Why would that matter?" Lilith asked. "A body is still a body."

Good use of words, Spalding thought. *She will make a fine Flesher.* "The White Hand might run illegal businesses, but they are businessmen. They don't wildly kill people. I don't know how they'd react if they found out how we got the bodies. Alastor and I always thought it was best we left the details out of the relationship."

"So B-b-Bran did it," Nox said.

"Maybe. We don't know, Nox," Spalding said. "What I do know is that Alastor and I were to deliver a new shipment to them this week. Now that task is in my hands."

"S-s-something set them off. It has to be Bran," Nox said.

"We shouldn't rule out all options," Spalding said. He knew that the boy was angry, blinded by his emotions and fixated on pointing the finger at anyone that seemed to be a likely candidate for the death. Alastor and Spalding created a complicated scenario with the White Hand, body-snatching and the murder of the Black Hand member, Donnie. It was a lot of information with no conclusion that would only confuse Nox. Alastor and Spalding had developed a good relationship with the White Hand, and he would hate to see it go to shit just because Nox was upset. They needed more answers.

"I w-w-want you to fill me in with everything that happens with the White Hand," Nox said.

"We will. You'll be up to speed in no time. Let me continue the relations with the White Hand, for now, considering we have a delivery to make. I'll confront them there, see what they know. If they don't have anything to say we'll leave them as-is."

"Wh-wh-what if they do?" Nox said.

"We'll take the right course of action. The White Hand run a tight ship. We will treat them as a suspect. We also won't destroy our relationship with them because of Alastor's death." *Not to mention Niles' secret love life,* Spalding thought. He wanted to bring it up with Nox, but it was a lot of information to fill the kid in on. There would be plenty of time to bring Nox up-to-date about everything Spalding and Alastor were up to. For now, it was best for Spalding to handle their relations with the White Hand. He was the only one at Rutherford Manor who knew the details of it.

"I should j-j-join you," Nox said.

Spalding wanted to laugh. The thought of Nox joining him was a bit amusing. What would Nox do? He couldn't fight. "I appreciate your courage, but I think you're a bit too young to be getting your hands this dirty."

"Of course," Nox said. Disappointment filled his tone. "What about Billy?"

"Does he know what we do?" Lilith asked.

"Not fully, but I'll fill him in," Spalding said. The suggestion was a pleasant surprise from the boy. Possibly the first official choice of business he made. "Good thinking, Nox. You truly have the mind of your father. You will do him proud."

Spalding took a bow and walked over to Billy. Vivian had left him; she was now beside her dead father, paying her respects.

"Billy," Spalding said.

"Yes, Spalding?" Billy asked.

"Your arrival at Rutherford Manor could not have been timelier," Spalding said.

"I don't follow."

"Alastor and I had some interesting work. With his passing, Nox is taking his place, but he is a bit premature to be involved in some of the tasks. How would you like to have a job?"

"I would," Billy said. "But I need to know more."

"You know those violent tendencies you have?"

"Yes."

"They might be of use to us. We're going to go hunting."

Billy smiled, a wicked smile from cheekbone to cheekbone. It even made Spalding feel a chill rattle down his spine.

CHAPTER 17

BEHIND THE CURTAIN

Grief. The natural human response to any tragic event. Each person behaves differently under the influence of this emotion. Some may internalize everything, while others might outwardly express it through action, such as violence. Regardless of how one chooses to express their sorrow, a trained eye is able to notice these signs. The trained eye can become empathetic, one that can identify and even sense a part of the pain that the grieving individual is feeling. For some of these empathetic souls, it can take a toll on their own conscience. How do you handle absorbing the grief of an entire family for the loss of their loved one?

Lilith stared at the backyard from the kitchen as the tea kettle began to boil on the burner. Her morning Earl Grey tea was mandatory if she wanted to get anything done in the day. She especially needed it after the emotionally heavy day that the family experienced the day before. Alastor's passing was not easy for anyone at Rutherford Manor. It left too many questions open. It was especially tricky for the Flesher children themselves.

My poor Nox, Lilith thought. She recalled how brave he was to give a speech at the funeral. It was an admirable act which gave her more respect for him. Unfortunately, she also knew Nox and knew the boy was internalizing a lot of the anger inside of him. She could sense it. Hell, even an unskilled eye could have seen the seed of fury that sprouted inside him that day. Nox would want his revenge. The question was, how far was he willing to go to have it? That was what worried Lilith.

Would the boy do something foolish in an expression of rage? Or would he keep himself stable? Lilith wanted to spend the time to comfort Nox, but also knew how he had to process a situation. After the funeral, Nox went down to the basement where he stayed for the night. At some point today, Lilith would have to check on him. Perhaps after her tea was made.

Lilith let out a sigh and stared at the kettle, waiting for it to whistle. Was time moving more slowly or was she impatient because of the emotional intensity over the past few days? Truthfully, it could be a mix of both; it was not like it mattered too much. The tea would be ready when it was ready. The spare time left her in her thoughts, recalling how she'd come to be here. Lilith had been pleased to meet Nox at the University of Chicago; they had a lot of similar interests and were so innocent. It seemed like decades ago now, when in reality it had only been about a year. So much can change in a year.

The acid . . . Alastor. . . , Lilith thought, playing the memories of the critical events through her mind. The situations that would have an imprint on Nox forever. Would it eventually consume him, or would he be able to grow from the tragedies? Maybe the latter path, with Lilith's help.

For herself, Lilith was oddly used to feeling such sorrow. She was also used to handling great heights of joy that others could only achieve on substances. The emotional rollercoaster of her sixth sense was a gift and a burden.

Mother would be so proud, Lilith thought. She remembered her mother telling her about the family's long history of connections with the afterlife. They were able to communicate with the dead and the supernatural. It was an alluring story. Her father never bought into the powers, but then again, most people didn't. The difficulty was in trying to prove it. Then you had the witch-hunts over the past several centuries. People weren't comfortable with the things they didn't understand.

On the contrary to the popular stance, Lilith thrived in the unknown. It kept her on her toes. When one becomes comfortable, they become lazy and rigid. Those were two traits that left a bad taste in her mouth. She was a Blum. Somehow, they were always involved with the fantastical.

Mother, if only you could see the type of world America is, she thought. Her family had always wanted to come to the West. Unfortunately, they never had the funds to do so. What little they did have, they pooled together for Lilith so she could continue her studies and take advantage of the New World. With all of the recent events, she would have to write them a letter soon. It had been a few months since her last one; there would be a lot to cover.

The kettle began to whistle, catching her eye just as the

creaking of wood—and footsteps—picked up. Vivian entered the room at a slow pace, head down and her doll tucked under her arm.

"Morning, Vivian," Lilith said while she took the kettle off of the burner. *Focus,* she thought while feeling an intense wave of emotion rush through her. Vivian's aura of sorrow was potent. The girl was still mourning the loss of her father and her being so near was distracting from the simple task of pouring tea into a pot. Lilith was used to these types of sense-waves. This was just a typical day for a Blum.

"Hi Lilith," Vivian mumbled while taking a cup out of the cupboard.

"Would you care for some tea?" Lilith asked.

"Yes please," she said while placing the cup beside Lilith's.

Lilith smiled at her while pouring the hot water into the teapot. "I can fix you one up then." *That poor girl,* Lilith thought. "How did you sleep?"

"Okay. Well, no. That is a lie. I didn't sleep well at all."

"Oh, my dear, I am so sorry to hear. Were you up all night?"

"Most of it. I wasn't alone at least."

"Was Tammy with you?" Lilith asked, glancing at the doll Vivian had.

"Yeah, Tammy was with us, and Billy was awake. He was kind enough to talk to me."

He's a good soul. Troubled, but good, Lilith thought. She'd detected compassion from the man when she first met him. As pure as the sensation was, she also felt a just-as-powerful shadow that followed him. Billy had skeletons, but who didn't? "I'm glad someone was with you. Billy has a good heart, I can feel it."

"Really?" Vivian said with a weak smile. "That is nice to hear. He is nice."

"Mind grabbing the cups for us?" Lilith asked as she took the teapot and plates to the dining room.

"Of course," Vivian said.

The two entered the empty dining room and sat side by side, waiting for the tea to steep. Lilith was always up before anyone else at Rutherford Manor. She was often the only one up when she was at university too. She enjoyed the mornings; they were quiet because everyone was locked into their dreams. It gave her emotions time to rest since no one was near.

"So, you just stayed up all night until someone was awake?" Lilith said with worry.

"Yeah, I heard the kettle and thought I would come to keep you company," Vivian said, stroking Tammy's hair.

"That's kind of you. I do appreciate some company," Lilith said. *A small lie,* she thought. Truthfully, Lilith liked the silence during the morning. But she was wise enough to know the difficulties Vivian was going through were far more important than a single morning of silence.

Vivian smiled. "Oh, good. I'm glad it's not a nuisance to you."

"Nonsense." Lilith took the teapot and poured both of them a cup. "You want help fetching up some breakfast for everyone?" she asked.

"You don't have any of your plants to take care of this morning?" Vivian asked while taking her cup.

"I already took care of them."

"Then sure, that would be of much help."

"Splendid," Lilith said. She began to sense Vivian's aura alter.

The waves it was radiating began to calm down, and there was a sense of ease. There was still sorrow, but it was stable. Lilith was a good distraction for the girl.

The two enjoyed their tea and chatted while finishing up the pot. Once Lilith and Vivian were done, they returned to the kitchen and began to prepare breakfast for the family. The sun was starting to rise, and that meant the household would be awake. Alastor used to be the early-morning riser. Now, Spalding was the first to get up. Times changed.

Lilith and Vivian fried up the eggs, sausages, and beans. It was a simple, hearty meal that could feed everyone. A pot of coffee helped too. Lilith had never been much for coffee, but the rest of the family seemed to enjoy those burnt beans.

Footsteps came from the hallway until Spalding appeared in the kitchen, resting his hands on the doorframe. His hair was combed back, his shirt buttoned. As per usual, he was cleaned up even before he came to socialize with the rest of the manor.

"Morning, ladies," Spalding said.

"Morning," Lilith called out while evenly distributing the breakfast items onto the plates.

"Breakfast is a bit early?" he asked.

"Well, neither of us could sleep well last night," Lilith said. "It has been an emotional past few days, and a breakfast like this should get everyone back on track."

"Fair enough," Spalding said while looking down the hall. "Did he ever come out from down there?"

Lilith knew that Spalding was referring to Nox. "No," she said. "He never did come up to bed." She placed the pan down on an unheated burner and then took the plates to the dining room.

Vivian grabbed the coffee pot while Spalding followed. "I'm sure he'll come out soon," he said.

Lilith let out a sigh and looked at the man. Spalding always had a calm presence. Internally conflicted, but calm. Even with Alastor's death, his aura seemed to stay the most stable out of everyone at the manor, next to Billy, who had no real connection to Alastor.

"I'll fetch Billy," Spalding said.

"I'll grab Nox," Lilith said.

"Good luck," Spalding said before leaving the room.

Lilith looked over at Vivian, who put on a closed smile. It was time to take the headmaster from his study.

Lilith exited the dining room and strolled down the staircase leading to the basement. She took a lantern with her, which provided the only light in the next room. A dim, yellow glow was seen down the hall. Either Nox was still awake, or the silly boy had fallen asleep with the light on—a dangerous situation if one wasn't careful where they placed it.

The girl walked down the hall slowly until she entered the main room of Nox's study. The operating table was empty; the tools were neatly placed on the tray beside it. The shelves and the floor were a bit messy with papers and contraptions, as per usual. Off to the right side was his desk with a lantern on top. Nox was hunched over the table with a pen and paper. He didn't even notice her come in.

The boy's presence projected powerful energy—a dark one that she had never really experienced before. She'd noticed Nox had a powerful aura during the funeral; it seemed to be a mix of sadness, fear and anger. Now, she could only feel the hate that radiated from him.

He must have been up all night, Lilith thought. She walked over to the desk, placed the lantern on top, and stepped behind Nox. She gently glided her hands down to the boy's shoulders, feeling the intensity of his being amplify with her touch.

"Nox," she said softly, looking down at the piece of paper. He was sketching out blueprints for something she hadn't seen before. It appeared to be some sort of metal glove, but the drafts were too early to really tell.

"Nox, it is morning," she said while rubbing his shoulders.

Nox stopped moving the pen. His hand froze for a moment before he dropped it onto the paper. His fingers shook for a moment before a howl erupted from him. His hands curled into fists as he began to sob, his head leaning against her forearm.

Lilith tightened her grip around the boy, embracing him in his sudden burst of sorrow. The intense aura of anger was now nothing but sadness. The rage of a young man was converted into the cries of a grieving son.

"It's okay, let it out," Lilith said while stroking his hair with her one hand. She continued to comfort him for several minutes as the boy cried. His tears ran down his face and soaked into her dress. That didn't matter; she had to hold him. He opened up to no one else.

"Wh-wh-why?" Nox slurred. "Why did he have to go?"

"I don't know," Lilith said. "It is a terrible, terrible, tragedy."

"He wasn't ready!" Nox's tears continued.

Lilith gently rocked him back and forth, trying to soothe him as he breathed erratically between his moments of sobbing.

"I can't do this," Nox said. "I c-can't fill the role that my father had."

"Nonsense," Lilith said. "You will do him proud."

"Father was a st-st-strong man. He was wise and compassionate. I don't have any of th-those traits."

"Do you think he did at your age?" Lilith asked.

Nox sniffled. "N-n-no, probably not."

"Exactly, you are being hard on yourself. No one expects you to be as grand as Alastor was. That level of wisdom and knowledge takes years to develop. You will learn and grow at your own rate and become a man equal to him. Right now, you will be you, your father's son. That is what he would expect and what everyone else expects from you."

"I don't kn-kn-know," Nox said.

"Yes, you do," Lilith said, rubbing his arms. "You have the right to grieve. No one would expect anything less from you."

"What am I supposed to do? L-l-lilith? What?"

"Keep doing this." Lilith pointed to the sketch on the table. "Your amazing work! This is the strength that you offer your family. Your ability to create and craft these inventions is something people only dream of doing. Your father greatly admired what you were able to do."

"It n-n-never felt like enough. All the pain that he had to go through. Th-th-the suffering he and Vivian had while I was g-g-gone to university. Walter never helped," Nox said.

"Well, this isn't about Walter," Lilith said. "From what I understand, he made his choice, and you made yours to come back to Rutherford Manor and help the family."

"Am I helping?" Nox asked.

"Of course you are. Your solution to immobilizing the snatch victims was genius. It made Alastor's and Spalding's work far easier, and they got better pay for the bodies."

"Th-th-that was your work too," Nox said.

"That is because we are a team. You on your own are great, and together we can bring Rutherford Manor to a new level. Trust me."

"I w-w-want to," Nox slurred. "I just f-f-feel a doubt deep in me. I can't do what Alastor and Spalding did. I'm not like others, Lilith. I'm different. Even before the accident, I never fit in."

"No, you don't," Lilith agreed while releasing the boy from her arms.

Nox stopped sniffling and turned to face her as she sat down on the desk. He had a look of confusion on his face.

"You're not like anyone else. Even at Rutherford Manor, a place for misfits, you stand out. That is also what makes you great."

Nox's unscarred half of his mouth expressed a weak smile. Lilith's words were resonating with him. She could sense his emotions begin to calm down. It took effort, but she was always able to bring his temper back to normal.

"Nox," Lilith said while stroking his face. "Your talent is what makes you shine. Your mind will be able to provide for the family."

"Is th-th-that enough?" Nox asked.

"Yes. But you are not alone in this. I am here. I always have been. You do not need to face this on your own. Have I ever led you astray?"

Nox shook his head no.

"Then why are you so full of doubt?" Lilith said with a smile.

Nox looked up at her, wiping the last few tears from his eyes. "I d-d-don't really know."

Lilith brought the boy in for a hug, pressing his head against her chest. "Then put your trust in me."

CHAPTER 18

CONFRONTATION

Another week, another job, and another long ride into Chicago. But this trip was not exactly like Spalding's other trips. This time he had Billy with him. And he couldn't be happier to have the man at his side when he was about to confront the White Hand about Alastor's death. Things could either go smoothly—presuming the gang had nothing to do with it—or head south very fast. The two of them might have to get into a messy fight.

Lilith and Nox provided them with the dope, as with every snatch. Spalding held on to it this time. It felt odd to carry the syringe that Alastor was usually in charge of. Everything was different now.

Billy had his own set of tools. His throwing hatchet, and a large knife intended to carve animals. Ideally, they wouldn't be gutting people tonight, but it never hurt to be prepared.

"What the hell is that?" Billy asked as they loaded the carriage.

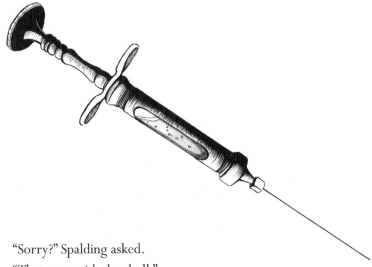

"Sorry?" Spalding asked.

"That cane with the skull."

"Oh!" Spalding looked over at Pierre, who rested flat on the side of the carriage. "That's Pierre, my friend."

"What is it doing here?"

"It's a respect thing. Unfortunately, I had to kill him. We were young and playing in the woods. He slipped, impaled himself on a branch, fell further and broke some bones. His howls of agony caught the attention of wolves. He begged me to end it."

"Sad."

Spalding nodded. "I never wanted it to end up that way. I wanted to fend off the wolves. I even snapped the branch so he could be more mobile. Pierre told me to not waste my time. He had lost a lot of blood. So, I took a nearby rock and beat him to death." Spalding's heart sunk; he hadn't shared the story with many people. It wasn't a pleasant one, and Spalding generally preferred to keep the mood positive.

"What's with the trinkets?"

"The stick itself was what impaled him. Crows were his favourite animals. He always wanted a pet crow, but his folks gave him the farm's chicken instead."

"That's not the same."

"No. No, it's not."

The two men finished loading the carriage and rode into Chicago in the evening. Spalding informed Billy about what they did, how they did it, and who they delivered it to. The trip to the big city sped by as Spalding shared all the information he had with Billy.

"So that's all of it?" Billy asked. "You and Alastor killed people for the study of anatomy and the White Hand killed Alastor out of disapproval about how you two get bodies?"

"That's a good summary, aye," Spalding said while puffing on a smoke. "We don't know that the White Hand did it, but I have a hunch that they were involved. They have their own secrets."

"Because of the Black Hand family?"

"Yeah, and Niles—he's one of their henchmen. You're actually the first person I've told about this, so let's keep it to ourselves for now until we've got more information about it all. Nox is a bit emotionally unstable."

"Fair enough," Billy said. "So, you slept with your boss's daughter?"

Spalding sighed. *Irene, that seductive woman.* "Yeah, she had a way with her words and her mannerisms. Something about her was like a vortex."

"She seduced you," Billy said.

"That's the simplified version," Spalding said.

"This is messy," Billy said.

"That it is."

Billy's matter-of-fact blunt statements were refreshing to hear. He offered a unique input into the tangled mess Spalding found himself in. Their ride into town proved to be a good sounding-board session.

"You're alright with"—Spalding paused—"killing someone today?"

"Yes. I said already. This is no different than a hunt."

"Good, just double-checking," Spalding said. "These aren't common activities."

"I'm not common," Billy said.

The two reached Chicago and rode the carriage through the streets. Spalding told them how they generally targeted a range of profiles to keep the product interesting for Bran. They profiled some of the people that walked down the street, discussing who could be their target.

"We tried to be random with the locations as well," Spalding said. "The last thing we need is the law having any interest in us. So far to date, we've been squeaky clean."

"No traces, understood," Billy said.

They parked the carriage and locked it. They were now ready to prowl the town. Dusk approached. The night would be their most opportune time to strike.

Spalding lit a cigarette. The whole packaged situation of his life oozed stress. He felt a burning urge to smoke and drink aggressively, then find a vazey gal for a brush. Would that help their situation? No. He had to stay in the game. Focused. He had to find out what happened to Alastor.

"What about that one?" Billy asked, nodding at a man walking down a quiet street on his own. There was a spring to his step. He was frail, like a bone rack. Young. Peppy. The streetlights cast soft shadows on him as he moved out of view.

"Possibly, why him?" Spalding asked.

"He's alone, young, probably doesn't have a family yet," Billy said. "He wouldn't be much trouble for us to take. This neighbourhood seems quiet."

"Not a bad choice; let's do it." Spalding usually was more cautious with their choice of snatch, but this time he didn't care. For all he knew, this would be their last snatch after meeting with the White Hand.

The two walked as one, initiating the hunt. Turning the corner, the man came into view. He didn't get far. The hunters followed at a slow pace, keeping about a half a block away. They couldn't be obvious with their stalking.

Billy had a stern gaze. His eyes locked onto the young man. His glare was different than Alastor's ever was. Emotionless. Empty. Focused. He was set on killing. A type of glare seen in someone stalking wildlife, ready to show no mercy. Spalding had seen that same look on the man's face before, at the fight club. Billy's curse.

The young man turned down an alleyway, now out of view. The street was still empty; this neighbourhood clearly didn't get a lot of action.

"That's it," Billy said as he picked up his pace to catch up with their target.

Spalding followed him as quickly as he could. Billy was fast and took the lead of the situation. The man wanted this. The two turned the corner of the alley to see that the young man kept walking, alone. Where was he going? Did it matter? They were moving quite fast; Spalding hadn't even had time to process it. There wasn't much of a plan.

"Okay, I'll ask him a question, and we can ambush him," Spalding said.

"How about this?" Billy pulled out his hatchet and brought his arm back in a single smooth motion. He leaned his arm back a little further. Pause. Throw. The hatchet soared down the alleyway, spinning rapidly, and pierced right into the man's skull. Their victim tumbled forward and faceplanted onto the gravel.

"Christ, Billy!" Spalding said.

"No one is watching. Hurry." Billy rushed down the alleyway to the body.

Spalding caught up to his comrade as Billy pulled the hatchet out of the man's skull. The body twitched as blood began to ooze out of his head.

"We don't have our carriage with us. It's a good three blocks away," Spalding said.

"I'll grab the carriage," Billy said. He eyed the alleyway; there were some garbage cans and stacked crates nearby.

Spalding glanced up and down the alley to check if they were still alone. Yes. This was either dumb luck, or Billy knew how to time his kills.

Billy snagged the man by the ankles and dragged him towards the garbage cans. "Stay by here," he said as he tucked the dead man behind the tins. "I'll return."

"Here," Spalding said while putting his hand in his pocket to fish out the carriage's lock keys and tossed them to his partner. Billy caught them and dashed out of the alley.

He really does like this stuff, Spalding thought. He shouldn't have been surprised that Billy was more gung-ho about this whole thing than Spalding was. Even after all these months, Spalding had issues with what he and Alastor did. Just because they did it on a weekly basis didn't mean it became 'the normal' for him. The cold-blooded killing was no better than the flesh consumption they had engaged in.

Spalding lit up a smoke. His last one, and he puffed on it repeatedly. A few people walked by the alleyway, but never down it. He was alone. The sun moved past the horizon and darkness covered the city. The alley was quite dark, with only the dim glow from the nearby streetlights. At least the night provided some coverage.

There he is, Spalding thought, feeling a wave of relief rush over him as the familiar carriage turned down the alleyway.

Billy got out of the carriage and hurried around back. He unlocked the back door and brought the large canvas sack over. The two men hastily grabbed the body from the alley, rolled him up, and dropped him into the back of the carriage. They hopped onto their ride and rolled off. Job complete.

"I have to say that is the fastest snatch I have done to date," Spalding said with a grin. "You're wild."

"Like I said, I have a curse. This is what I cannot control. The hunt constantly calls to me."

"Well, save some of that energy for when we confront the White Hand," Spalding said.

"Of course," Billy said.

The blood, Spalding thought. What if someone noticed the blood the next day? It didn't matter, really. No one saw the murder and Billy had used a hatchet—a clean way of killing. There were no cries of pain, no gunpowder residue. The snatch was complete. Pierre didn't even get to make an appearance.

They lit the lantern on the carriage and rode out of Chicago. Onward to the regular meeting point with the White Hand. Spalding felt his heart race. This was the moment of truth. They could confront Bran about Alastor.

Billy and Spalding were first to arrive at the rendezvous. Rightfully so, considering how quick the kill was. Spalding remained in his own thoughts as they waited. He didn't have anything to say and felt it was best to wait in silence, watching. Billy knew the situation; he knew what they looked like, and what had to be done. Now, they waited.

Not for long. Four horses trotted up the hill and approached them with riders wearing wide-brimmed hats. Niles on the left, Bran after, and Blyton on the other side. The last gangster, a lady, also wore a hat. Irene.

A cocktail of emotions rattled up in Spalding. Anger. Uncertainty. Fear. Pain. A volatile mixture. The one woman he had troubles removing from his mind and the gang who could have insight into his dead friend's murder were all in front of him in one grand finale.

"Spalding," Bran said as the horses came to a stop. He dismounted slowly and put his hands on his belt. "I expected to see you with Alastor. Who is this?"

"I thought I could ask you the same thing, Bran," Spalding said. *A bit too much to the point,* Spalding thought. He didn't want to come here and start making accusations about them. He was here to conduct business and glean information. For now.

"I don't follow," Bran said.

The other three White Hand members dismounted and all four walked up to Spalding and Billy. They had their hands by their belts, near their holstered weapons, stances wide. They were already on the defensive.

"Nothing," Spalding said. "This is Billy. He is filling in."

"Evening," Billy said.

"No, that is *not* nothing," Bran snarled. "I don't appreciate sly remarks, Spalding. And this is beginning to look quite suspicious."

Well, I fucked that up, Spalding thought.

Irene glared at Spalding with a smirk on her face.

Ignore her, Spalding thought. *Why is she smiling? Did she do something?*

Spalding looked over at Billy, who kept his gaze on the four newcomers. His breath was steady, like he was about to enter the ring at the fight club. Billy was ready. Spalding had known this was coming. It was time to rumble . . . for Alastor.

"Grab 'em!" Bran ordered.

Billy and Spalding dashed forward as the White Hand members drew their weapons. Spalding raised his fists, rushing towards Irene. She pulled out a pistol and fired as Spalding snagged her wrist, re-directing the bullet into the air.

A scream erupted, and heavy thumping sounds came from where Billy was.

Spalding didn't have time to look as he knocked Irene's wrist back toward her, slamming her own gun into her face. The blow disoriented her, probably broke her nose. She let go of the weapon in the process.

A sharp jab went into Spalding's shoulder; he grunted and stepped away from Irene. He held onto the gun tightly, shifting his stance from Irene to see Niles now stood beside her. Spalding took a step back, away from his new opponent.

Behind Niles lay Blyton on the ground in a pool of his own blood, innards spilled out like a butchered pig. Billy dashed from the corpse towards Bran, who fired at him. The bullet grazed his shoulder but didn't stop the man.

Niles rushed towards Spalding, knife raised high. Spalding cocked the gun.

"Stop!" came Bran's commanding voice.

Niles froze in mid-swing down to Spalding's neck. Spalding had his finger on the trigger, pointing the gun to Niles' chest. Stalemate.

"Stop," Bran said.

Spalding took a step back while pointing the gun into the air, showing all ten fingers.

Niles showed his palms as well and stepped back to Irene, who rubbed her bloody face.

"Mind dropping the knife?" Bran said.

Spalding looked over to see Billy had Bran in a chokehold with the blood-dripping hunting knife to his throat. The red liquid stained his suit.

"Daddy—Ahem, Bran. . . ," Irene said in a high-pitched voice. Daddy's girl. Irene's soft spot.

"Okay, Bran," Spalding said while circling around Niles and Irene towards Billy and Bran. "We need answers."

"You really are that stupid, aren't you?" Bran asked. "Alastor is the mind behind this, isn't he? You're simply the dimwitted goon."

"*Is* his mind behind this?" Spalding asked. "You mean he *was*? Am I not wrong?"

"Fine!" Bran hissed. "You're beating around the bush trying to get me to say I did it. Alastor is dead; I got that when I arrived here. But I'm not confessing to something I didn't do."

"Sorry?" Spalding said, walking up to Bran, who was only a couple feet away.

"Like I said, you really are stupid. I had nothing to do with Alastor's death. Shit, I didn't even know about it until you showed up with this psycho. Blyton is dead!"

"Eye for an eye?" Spalding said. He wanted to keep badgering the man. He didn't want to buy the words he was saying. Bran had always been honest. Vague, but honest. The truth was hard to swallow.

"There is no eye for an eye, ratbag," Bran snarled.

"So, you're not lying? No bad blood between you and Alastor?" Spalding asked.

"No! Why would I?" Bran said.

"Perhaps Alastor was pushing you for more payment?" *Or that I fucked your daughter.* "Or you found out something about us you're not fond of."

"No!' Bran said again. "I have a hunch about how you get these bodies. They're still warm, for Christ's sake. That doesn't mean there was any bad blood with Alastor. I was fond of the man, actually. So, you see, I have no need to lie to a couple of low-life resurrectionists. And I certainly didn't need to waste my time killing Alastor."

"Okay," Spalding said. "Say that is the case, why was he going to meet you in town about five days ago?"

"Meet me?" Bran said. "No, we weren't going to meet. I'm afraid Alastor lied to you."

Spalding swallowed a thick lump of saliva in his mouth. This wasn't going anywhere. Bran was a dead end.

"Alastor was not dealing with any White Hand I know of," Bran said. "And in case you have forgotten, I am the top in Chicago, and you're beginning to piss me off."

Spalding looked at Billy, who glanced up at him.

Bran snorted. "It's bad enough dealing with the Black Hand seeking revenge for something we didn't do. Now you two are accusing us?"

The Black Hand. Donnie, Spalding thought. Bran's comment was more generalized, but Spalding knew the reason why the rival gang were putting pressure on the White Hand. Irene had confirmed it.

"Do the Black Hand know about our business?" Spalding asked. The question was a fish, but he was running out of ways to extract information from Bran. He couldn't tell the man that he and Alastor were responsible for the added heat from the Black Hand.

Bran shook his head. "No. They didn't get into body snatching. We do tend to cross territories in Chicago, which results in some folk dying. Then an all-out gang war breaks out."

The Black Hand still think the White Hand killed Donnie, Spalding thought. This wasn't going anywhere. His gaze shifted to Irene and Niles. "Well," Spalding said, waving the gun carelessly at

Niles and Irene, "you two have any insight into this?"

Niles looked down sheepishly as Irene stepped forward. "No," she said. "We didn't have anything to do with this. You two fools brought the bodies, and we paid you. It was pretty simple . . . until now."

"Nothing at all?" Spalding asked. "Nothing about love?"

"Have you gone delusional? We smuggle bodies," Irene said.

"Does the Black Hand spark any memory?" Spalding asked.

Niles looked up at him, pressing his lips together.

"Irene, what is he talking about?" Bran asked.

"Nothing, Bran," Irene said. "I really am as lost as you."

"Have you gone mad, Spalding?" Bran asked.

Liars, Spalding thought. As it was, they weren't getting anywhere, and this really was a complete waste of time. Irene and Niles weren't going to talk. Unless they took drastic measures with Bran's life. Spalding needed him, though. He provided their income and now they looked like idiots in front of him. *I'll meet Irene and Niles again, on less tense terms.* "Billy," Spalding said, "let him go."

Billy released Bran and stepped back from the man.

"Good," Bran said while adjusting his jacket. "Alastor is dead; that means his son has taken over the family business. What was his name again?"

"Nox," Spalding said.

"I'm going to stretch my suspicions further and say he put you up to this. The sad boy looking for revenge for his father's death." Bran chuckled. "Pitiful. Put the pieces together, Spalding. Why would Alastor go and meet me? You're his business partner. Was there something wrong with our arrangement?"

"No, can't say that there was. That's why it was odd," Spalding said.

"Tell you what," Bran said taking a step towards Spalding. "I'll forgive this hiccup, write it off as Nox's ill judgement as an adolescent. I haven't even met the kid and, quite frankly, I don't care to. I've done business with you, and let's keep it at that."

"Alright," Spalding said.

"You did bring a body, yes?" Bran said.

"Yes," Spalding said.

"We'll take it, but for free, understood? As payment for killing one of my men."

"Perfectly fair," Spalding said. *He's swift,* he thought. If things hadn't turned so sour so quickly, he could have learned a few things about negotiation from this man.

Bran extended his hand, saying, "And give my daughter's gun back."

Spalding was hesitant at first. What if Bran were to shoot him? Unlikely after the words he'd spoken. They'd best try and mend this relationship, or the family was going to go back to frying up human thighs. He surrendered the gun to Bran and took a step back.

"Good," Bran said, passing the gun to Irene.

"Thank you," Irene said, staring at Spalding with slanted brows and a twisted nose. Rage.

Brat, Spalding thought.

"Let's get these folks their body," Spalding said while walking to the carriage. Billy sheathed his hunting knife and snagged the key ring from his belt. The two unlocked the back door and pulled out the body.

"Good. We'll take it from here," Bran said.

Irene and Niles took hold of the wrapped-up body and hauled it to their horses, swinging it over one of the saddles and strapping it up.

Bran looked down at Blyton's gutted corpse before mounting his horse. "Same time next week. Don't bring any more surprises."

"Certainly," Spalding said.

"Hiya!" Bran shouted, causing his horse to dart away. Niles and Irene followed on their horses, leaving Spalding and Billy alone.

"That wasn't what we wanted," Billy said.

"No, that was not at all," Spalding said. "Dammit!" He kicked the dirt and took off his hat to wipe the sweat.

"You were stabbed," Billy said.

"Aye, nothing big. You were shot. We'll take care of it when we're back."

"Nox isn't going to be happy," Billy said.

"Not at all. Nor am I. Let's just be grateful that this relationship can carry on despite our screwup."

"Bran is a quick thinker. Why does he want us?"

"Well, they have the connections to the anatomists. We get the bodies. My guess is they upsell the bodies drastically to make it worth their time. They only need to be middlemen while we do the grunt work."

"I see," Billy said. "So next week we hunt again?"

"It would appear so," Spalding said.

The two closed up the carriage and hopped on. No one cared to move Blyton's body. Nature would take its course with that one.

CHAPTER 19

SOME THINGS CHANGE, OTHERS STAY THE SAME

Books. A powerful resource that can transcribe ideas from one mind to another. A real form of magic. You can absorb so much knowledge from one, and then another, and another! That was why they were so valuable. Alastor was one who admired books; they kept his brain sharp, and he never stopped learning. It was a trait that Nox inherited, with his constant state of curiosity.

The books that his father kept lined the walls of the man's former study. There had to be hundreds of them. It was a beautiful sight. Nox always wanted to dig into them and absorb all of the knowledge that he could. There was just never enough time.

Nox pulled each book off the shelf one by one, taking a peek at their cover designs and titles before tucking them back into the section. The man had tomes on everything: psychology, science, survival, philosophy, religion, witchcraft . . . the list went on.

The boy pulled on one book; removing it brought a flattened cloth scroll out with it as well.

Odd, Nox thought. Usually, loose papers weren't kept with his father's books. What was unique about this one? Nox tucked the book back in and pulled out the scroll. He pulled on the lace keeping it tied and unrolled the cloth. The fabric was covered in ancient-looking glyphs written in dark red.

What is this? Nox thought while eying the scroll, which presented an illustration of bird wings attached to a robed woman. Her face was elongated with well-defined cheek bones and black, reptilian eyes. Her arms were held upward, palms flat, fingers ending in claws. The left hand held a human skull. The right hand held coins, an apple and was draped in pearls. The illustration was encompassed by several circles, outlined with more mysterious glyphs. The whole drawing was a bit unsettling. Nox had never seen anything like it. What could have Alastor been up to?

Nox took a seat on the red reading chair beside him and tossed the cloth onto the table. *My father, the man of many secrets,* he thought. He spun the globe that rested on the table and gazed into the world as it moved around and around. He wasn't exactly sure why he was spinning the sphere. At least it helped pass the time. Sitting in his father's study was a heavy burden. Plus, he could continually feel his innards twist, anxious to know how Spalding and Billy's journey to the city and subsequent meeting had gone. With any luck, they wouldn't end up dead like his father.

How am I going to fill your shoes, Father? Nox thought, taking a seat back in the chair. He stared blankly at the books on the top shelf. *You knew so much; you read so much. Wisdom, power, and strength flowed through you. My last living parent.* He began to whimper uncontrollably, and a tear came down his cheek. He sniffled and fought back the remaining tears from falling down his face. No more crying. He had to be a man now, a strong leader of the Flesher clan.

I will marry Lilith, Nox thought. *I will be a good husband to her. We will continue the Flesher bloodline.* These were big goals. Being a caring and strong husband was a challenging task. Thankfully, his father had given him a good role model in his treatment of Nox's mother. It was an excellent example to mimic.

A knock came from the door, causing Nox to sit upright. "C-c-come in," Nox said, wiping his face.

Spalding came around the corner. He wore an undershirt, no top hat and had his arm in a bandage.

"What h-h-happened to you?" Nox asked.

"Just a scuff."

"Was it Bran?" Nox asked.

Spalding put his hands on his belt and shook his head. "No. Bran had nothing to do with this."

Nox's face twitched as he clutched his teeth. The words were like daggers that pierced into his heart. He let out a roar and swatted the decelerating globe, knocking the heavy metal ball onto the floor with his forearm. The blow flicked the ritual cloth off the table. It slid onto the wooden floor in between the two men.

Spalding stared at the cloth on the floor. "I didn't buy it at first either. But after talking Bran through the scenario, I know it wasn't him."

"How?" Nox said. "It h-h-has to be him! Lilith sensed it to be poison."

"She suggested it, if I recall."

Nox wanted to shout at Spalding. How dare he insult Lilith's judgement? He was right, though; Lilith had never used those exact words. She only *thought* it was poison based on her sixth sense.

"I don't think murder should be ruled out," Spalding said. "Lilith did feel something, and the situation is just too bizarre."

"Wh-wh-what did my father s-s-say before he left?"

"He was going to meet Bran and settle some business. But Bran confirmed he never had a meeting planned. Alastor lied to us."

Father, Nox thought. *Why would you lie? What were you hiding?*

"So whatever Alastor was doing, he didn't want to explain it to us," Spalding said.

"Wh-wh-why? You're his partner," Nox said.

Spalding shrugged. "I struggled with him about that all the time. It really didn't seem to matter to him."

"Th-th-this isn't over," Nox said.

"No. For now, all we know is that Alastor was out to meet someone," Spalding said.

"It has to be the White Hand. Th-th-they're the only ones who he has been closely involved with. Everyone else feared him."

"Well," Spalding said. "He had a few folks that weren't too fond of him."

"Like who?" Nox asked.

"Sheriff Jenson was always suspicious."

"H-h-he found Father's body."

"True; I'm just listing names off the top of my head. Walter is another who despised him."

"That is true," Nox said.

"There was that old lady in Rowley, the one who owns the flower shop."

"Mrs. Smalley? I d-d-don't think so."

"No, she is too old and incapable of such acts."

None of it added up. Spalding didn't have a clue. Nox didn't either. Their best guess had turned out to be a dead end. What was left to do now? The two remained quiet for several moments, lost in their thoughts.

"Nox," Spalding said. "We'll figure this out."

"Wh-wh-what do we do until then?" Nox asked.

"I think it's best we focus on mending Rutherford Manor. Your father's death has taken a great toll. It's on you and I to keep this household afloat."

"And the White Hand?"

"It'd be best if we keep business as per usual. I do have to tell you that they aren't too fond of us right now. Billy and I accidentally killed one of their men during the brawl."

Nox wasn't sure if he was supposed to feel something for the dead man or if that was just Spalding giving him information about what happened. He remained silent, as he often did when people said something that he couldn't fully process.

"I'll try and repair the relationship. Billy will accompany me with the snatchings, and we'll pull in some more income for the household," Spalding said. "We'll also get you caught up on how the whole operation works."

"Th-th-that sounds good," Nox said. "I need to learn how my father worked."

"You will learn," Spalding said.

"Spalding, I have been th-th-thinking. Lilith and I have some unique talents. Father always said we could put them to use. I want to learn how to sell them."

"Sell your talents?" Spalding asked. "You mean your inventions?"

"Yes, I th-think it could be a good way to earn a living."

"I agree. You know, your father and I also discussed about saving enough cash from this resurrectionist business and opening up a butcher shop. Earn a legitimate living instead."

"Th-th-that sounds fair. I want to keep researching."

"I don't want to snatch bodies." Spalding extended his hand to Nox. "Sounds like we've made our first course of action as partners."

Nox smiled at him and shook his hand. Spalding squeezed it and yanked Nox's arm up and down. The sudden stern shake shocked the young Flesher momentarily before he recovered.

"We'll work on your handshake too," Spalding said. "So, I heard you proposed to Lilith? When's the wedding?"

"W-w-we want to do it soon. Now that all of the troubles with my father's death are sort of behind us, we're going to start making arrangements. Maybe in a month."

"No wasting time, I see." Spalding gave a slight bow. "Congratulations, Mr. Flesher."

"Th-th-thank you, Spalding." Hearing Spalding speak such words felt encouraging. Spalding had always treated Nox like a kid before. They had a bit of an age difference. Spalding was more like a second older brother. Now, he spoke to him directly, like they were working together. And they *were* working together, as partners. The new age of Rutherford Manor had begun.

CHAPTER 20

EXPOSED

Each day that passed at Rutherford Manor was a struggle. Most of the folk were focused on their duties, working together and making sure they could pick up the pieces following Alastor's death. Everyone knew there was no answer yet to explain what happened to him. This brought no resolution and left a lingering discomfort amongst everyone. This was not justice. Alastor did not deserve to fade away without closure to his death. How could anyone in the manor allow this to happen?

I have to confront Niles, Spalding thought daily.

A week went by. Then another. Still, no more clues about Alastor's death. It wasn't fair. The lack of any answers made one question whether there was any higher power taking care of them. Faith wasn't a topic that commonly came to Spalding's mind. He saw little proof of it in their own lives. The Savidges and Fleshers were always just scraping by. The concept of religion wasn't worth Spalding's time. He was too busy trying to survive or clean up messes that the Fleshers had created. Unfortunately, this time Spalding wondered if he was part of the chaos. If he had simply been stern with Alastor, perhaps the man would still be alive. If he'd refused to kill Donnie and his wife or persisted in joining his partner the night he vanished, everyone might be in a different scenario.

Sadly, there was no going back. There was only going forward. Spalding would do as he always did—try and outrun his mistakes. Maybe attempt to clean some of them up in the process.

Niles, Spalding thought, sipping on a cold ale in the basement of a hotel. He was glad to be away from his troubles for a little while and enjoy the fight club's sportsmanship. He watched as a couple men brawled with each other in the main fight ring. Folks roared as they cheered for their preferred candidate, hoping to win a bet.

Where are you? Spalding thought, scanning the crowd.

"Not interested in fighting this week?" Billy asked. He rested his arms on the table they sat at.

"Nah, still not really in the mood. That knife stab was a bit deep," Spalding said.

"That's not the case," Billy said.

"What do you mean?" Spalding asked.

"You've just been watching the crowd for the past several weeks. You're not focused on the fights at all."

"No," he admitted. *Good eye, Billy.* "No, I can't really enjoy the fight club right now."

"You're looking out for Irene?"

Irene, that seductive gal. "Aye, and Niles. Those two haven't shown up for a while."

"They know we go to the fight club. Given what happened you shouldn't be surprised that they've been avoiding it."

"I need to see them. They know something, Billy. You saw how they acted when we confronted Bran. Irene took the lead. Niles was brushing a Black Hand lady back in the summer. I believe all this has to be related to Donnie's death."

"It certainly makes sense," Billy said.

"Spalding!" shouted a manly voice. He was instantly recognizable by his mustache. Jacob waved at Spalding and Billy as he approached the table. "You still just watching?" The man raised his beer glass at him, and the two clanged their pints.

"Aye, that knife wound was a bit much," Spalding said.

"You're getting yourself into trouble, sir," Jacob said.

"I know, I know. Anyway, how are things with you? Win any fights?"

"I did last week, as you saw, but I'm keeping it low today too. Just observing."

"Oh? How come?" Spalding asked.

"I've got a big deal potentially going through tomorrow. I don't need to have my face beaten up."

"Big deal?" Spalding asked.

"Yeah," Jacob said. "Selling some land just outside of Rowley. Some folks are looking to start up a farmstead."

"You sell land?" Billy asked.

"Sure do. Real estate is my living. It's why I don't always fight. A bruised-up face is not the best way to make a first impression on a potential buyer."

"Real estate, huh?" Spalding leaned forward. "What type of

land do you sell?"

"All sorts. Are you looking to buy?"

"In due time. I'm saving up some cash to open up a butcher shop in Rowley here. Can you help with that?"

"Why yes, I can. How about you stop by my office tomorrow, and we can chat?"

Spalding put on a soft smile. The news created a mixture of excitement and sorrow inside of him. The butcher shop plan was initially birthed with Alastor. It was supposed to be their goal, together. Now he found himself carrying out the dream on his own.

Alastor, you secretive fool, Spalding thought. "That sounds splendid. What time?"

"How does shortly past noon sound?"

"Wonderful."

Jacob extended his hand and Spalding shook it firmly. "Good!" Jacob said. "My office is just across the street from the town hall; you can't miss it."

"Looking forward to it, friend."

"Likewise," Jacob said. "I'm going to catch the fight. Cheers." Jacob raised his glass and left the table.

"Well, Billy," Spalding said, "that could line up nicely with ending this resurrectionist gig."

"You didn't know he sold land?"

"No. We come here and brawl. It never occurred to me to ask what he does for a living. He has never asked me either."

"Yes. I suppose no one cares to know what I do."

"That is one of the perks of this fight club; we're all on equal levels here. The outside world doesn't really matter." Spalding took a big gulp of his drink, finishing the beer. Jacob's surprise conversation was good news. It brought the butcher shop dream one step closer to reality. Now they just had to save up the rest of the cash.

Probably a good year or two out, Spalding thought. The funeral costs had set them back financially, prolonging the goal of quitting the body-snatching gig. It didn't matter, though. Alastor deserved a proper burial.

"Spalding," Billy said.

"Aye?"

"Look." Billy pointed casually to the basement staircase where a man and woman, dressed in suits, had just arrived. Niles and Irene. The sight of the two caused Spalding's stomach to twist. His hair stood up on end and his eyes locked onto the two White Hand members as they entered the club.

"Goddammit, they finally show their faces," Spalding said. *They're finally here.*

"What do you want to do?" Billy asked.

"We need to confront them," Spalding said. "Wait until they're near us. We'll cut them off and keep it civil."

Billy and Spalding kept an eye on Niles and Irene as they moved throughout the busy crowd. Each step the White Hand took brought them closer to the two of them. The mobsters hadn't noticed them yet, thankfully. Their table was in the back of the room, and they kept their heads low.

"Okay, let's circle around them," Spalding said.

Both men got up from the table and hurried around the outskirts of the crowd. They kept an eye on the wide-brimmed hats that bobbed up and down through the sea of people. Billy and Spalding came parallel to the mobsters and weaved their way into the cluster of bodies. The two stepped past the last person and came face to face with the White Hand.

Niles and Irene froze in their steps. Irene placed her hand on her gun holster. Her crooked nose was more prominent with the sharp shadows of the limited lighting.

"Hold up," Spalding said, extending his hand. "We're not looking for a showdown."

"This is the fight club," Billy said. "Fights are for the ring."

Irene relaxed her posture.

Niles folded his arms. "Then what do you two want?"

"We need to clear the air," Spalding said. "Mind sitting with us?"

Niles and Irene exchanged looks, and Irene said, "Let's hear what they have to say."

"Thank you," Spalding said. *Keep it civil,* he thought as he led the group back to the table. Spalding wanted nothing more than to yell at the White Hand, blame someone for Alastor's death. He couldn't. He had to remain calm and polite if he wanted to get any information out of them. Force had gotten them nowhere last time.

"Okay," Niles said as all four sat down. "Are you coming to apologize for that mess?"

"Not quite," Spalding said.

"You almost ratted me out to my boss," Niles said. "Truthfully, I'm a bit pissed."

"As am I," Irene said, folding her arms. "You fucked my face up."

"Does that count as a second brush?" Spalding grinned.

"Enough." Billy slammed his hand down on the table. "We need answers. You two need explanations."

"Okay," Niles said. "You start then."

Spalding leaned forward, saying, "The Black Hand affair. Irene, you know about Niles' lover. What are you two hiding?"

Niles sighed. "I told you, Spalding. She died back in the summer."

"How?" Spalding asked.

"I don't know," Niles said.

"Was she Donnie's wife?" Spalding asked.

Irene squinted. "What do you know about Donnie?" she asked.

"You brought up his name and death," Spalding said. *Play stupid,* he thought. If Niles and Irene had any connection to Alastor's death, they would know that Alastor and Spalding were responsible for Donnie's murder, the gang dispute, and the death of Niles' lover. "You two and Bran keep mentioning heat from the Black Hand."

"Yeah," Irene said. "That mess is just about taken care of."

"Okay. They blame you for Donnie's death. Why?"

"We're the obvious ones," Niles said. "We're their direct rival. Donnie had some weight in Chicago, so they're angry. We've chased them back to their side of town, though."

"Okay, back to my original question," Spalding said. "Is your lover Donnie's wife?"

"No," Niles said. "The two situations aren't related."

"Really?" Spalding asked. "She and Donnie both just happened to die in the summer?"

"Yeah," Niles said.

"How did she die?"

"Like I said, I don't know," Niles said.

"How do you know she's dead?" Spalding asked.

Irene cleared her throat. "The Black Hand found out about their affair."

"That was the last thing she told me," Niles said, looking to the ground. "I'd presume she is dead. They aren't forgiving."

Spalding leaned back. "What was her name?" he asked.

"Isabel," Niles said. "What does this have to do with Alastor's death?"

Spalding looked over at Billy, who stared at Niles. They weren't getting anywhere. Was Niles telling the truth? Was it just a coincidence that the deaths were in the same season?

"When did you last see your lover?" Spalding asked.

Niles locked eyes with Spalding. "Why does that matter?" he asked. "What is your point here?"

"Did you kill Alastor?" Spalding asked.

"No," Niles said. "I did not."

Spalding looked over to Irene.

She shook her head. "No."

Billy leaned forward. "Do you know anything about it?" he asked.

"Can't say we do," Niles said, staring into Spalding's eyes. "It is unfortunate to hear you suffered such a loss. If anything, I hope you understand a bit of the pain I am going through."

Spalding sighed, a heavy exhale of defeat. What did this mean? *Alastor, what happened to you?* Spalding thought.

"Our turn," Irene said. "What's your deal with Niles' lover and Alastor's death?"

Spalding shrugged. "Just trying to piece this thing together," he said.

"Why Donnie and Niles' lover, though?" Irene asked. "All three of these cases are unrelated."

"They all happened roughly around the same time," Spalding said. It was the best answer he could come up with. Niles and Irene couldn't know the truth. With any luck, they'd buy it.

Irene shook her head. "You're a damned loose cannon, Spalding. That stunt you pulled was complete bullshit."

"Aye," Spalding said, sulking into his chair. He felt sheepish facing another failed attempt at unravelling Alastor's death and having Irene scold him. She was still aggravated with him for breaking her nose. He wondered if he could mend things with her.

"Are you two going to pull any more of that rubbish on us?" Irene asked.

"No," Billy said.

"Have we made it clear we have nothing to do with your friend's death?" Irene said.

"Yes," Spalding said.

Niles folded his arms. "We didn't want bad blood between us. I understand how you came to the conclusion of accusing us. We've proven ourselves innocent."

You just gave your word, Spalding thought. He wanted to challenge them, but they were entering a blame game. Maybe Niles was telling the truth. The two in front of them seemed to have their story straight. Bran had clearly been confused by their harsh accusations. The White Hand's involvement with Alastor's death was proving to be a dead end. Maybe Spalding was just jumping to conclusions.

"You boys going to behave?" Irene asked.

"Yeah, let's call a truce?" Spalding said, sitting upright.

"Truce," Niles said.

Irene nodded. "Good. We're done here, then?"

"Aye," Spalding said.

"Good evening, then," Niles said as he and Irene got up from the table and proceeded to vanish into the crowd.

"Nox isn't going to be pleased," Billy said.

"He doesn't know about this hypothesis," Spalding said, watching as Irene and Niles walked away. "I didn't want him to until we cleared this possibility." *Irene,* he thought. Even though all the violence and miscommunication, that gal was one of a kind. What was his obsession with her? Besides the obvious charm and looks she had? *She knows me,* Spalding thought. It hadn't been clear to him until now why he was so infatuated with this girl. Irene knew Spalding. Other gals only saw him on the surface. He was persuasive, attractive and effective with his hands—traits that look good on the outside. But none of those women really knew who he was. Irene knew he had a dark side to his life. She was the kind of lady that he could have more than a fling with. A wife? Maybe that was too soon to know. He would never know unless he made a move.

"Wait!" Spalding got up from his chair and hurried to the two mobsters. He gently grabbed Irene's arm, causing her and Niles to turn around.

"Irene," Spalding said. "Can I have a moment with you?"

"I got this," Irene said to Niles.

Niles rolled his eyes and stepped away into the crowd.

Irene's piercing eyes shot at Spalding like bullets. That deep gaze she had. The one that sucked him in every time. "What do you want, Spalding?" she asked.

"I. . . ." Spalding paused. What was he to say? Ask if she'd be his wife? No way. He wasn't very familiar with following up with women. Hopping to the next lady was his normal game. "I, I want to apologize for everything."

"You realize what you did to my nose?" Irene hissed.

"I know, I messed a lot up. Can I repay you?"

Irene began to laugh. "Who do you think you are?"

"Spalding," he said with a grin. "Who else would I be?"

Irene shook her head and smiled, amplifying the shape of her dimple. "You are a goddamned charmer. The looks complement it well too."

A heavy thud erupted inside of Spalding's rib cage. His heart, what did it just do? Her words had struck something inside him. "Irene. . . ." Spalding gently took her hand, pulling her towards him. *What are you doing?* he thought as he leaned into her. This was the daughter of Bran, the head of Chicago's White Hand. Their relationship was already a mess, and here he was wooing the man's daughter. This was crazy.

Irene shut her eyes as their faces closed in. Spalding did the same, ready to embrace her soft touch. His lips collided with skin, backed by something solid and bumpy. Wait—that was not her lips.

"Spalding," Irene said.

Spalding opened his eyes to see his lips met with her fingers.

"You're cute," she said with a smirk, breaking free from his grasp. "See you around." Her hand slid from his lips, ending in a pluck of his lower lip. She turned around and strolled off into the crowd, leaving him alone. He always was alone. But unlike previous affairs, this was not by choice.

ACT IV

Depression

CHAPTER 21

NUMBERS DWINDLE

Change. The one constant in the universe that can be agreed upon. Nothing stayed the same, except for the fact that change was guaranteed. But that didn't make it easier when the shift did occur. It could take months, if not years to become accustomed to something new. Especially if the change was so deeply rooted in the core of a household, like a family member's death. Changes like those linger in the air forever and do not leave the thoughts and hearts of those who live there. The loss of a great leader and a loving father is too much to live and forget. An alteration like that is never easy to come to terms with. It is permanent.

Alastor's death had affected Rutherford Manor in that way in the years that passed. The families continued their normal routine, adjusting to the new headmaster. He wasn't quite as commanding as his father. It was a substantial shift in the beginning. Nox had to learn—quickly—about the inner workings of how to keep Rutherford Manor alive. His sister, Vivian, continued to do a lot of the housekeeping and Lilith helped her from time to time. Lilith, Nox's wife. She was more focused on growing her plants and collaborating with Nox's projects. She was far more effective with her brain than in doing simple maintenance tasks—no offence to his sister.

Spalding and Billy continued the resurrectionist side of the business to raise enough money so they could cut their ties with the White Hand entirely. Spalding kept Nox informed about what each snatch was like on a weekly basis. This way, Nox could learn how Spalding dealt with the gang. Spalding and Billy were no more than vendors supplying their buyer with the goods they needed.

Nox was persistent in finding ways to develop other streams of income. He could almost taste blood every time Spalding or Billy mentioned Bran or the White Hand. Even though they had no proof, he knew they were involved with Alastor's death. He couldn't let that fact go. No one else had answers. The sheriff had basically written the whole thing off as a heart attack and never even looked at the blatantly obvious clues.

As he walked down the path in the forest, a leaf fell down onto the ground in front of Nox. He stopped on the gravel trail and looked down at it. The leaf was entirely green, yet it had fallen from the branch. Yellow leaves were supposed to descend from trees. Seeing a green one drop in this way was a little unusual. Green meant it was healthy. Why did it fall? Why did Nox's father fall? Even in his old age, the man was strong. That was how Nox knew it wasn't a heart attack, it was a murder.

Father, Nox thought, staring at the leaf. *Am I doing you proud now that I am a man?* he thought. *Three years on and I can't get you out of my head.* Pride was the force behind the question—the same question—that Nox asked himself every time he thought of his father. He repeatedly worried that he was not living up to Alastor's name.

Spalding had to continually remind Nox that he was only twenty-four years old and Alastor was close to his sixties at the time of his death. Alastor had lived Nox's life three times over and had all the experience under his belt. Naturally the father's life experience had far surpassed that of his child.

"As long as you keep at it, you'll be like your father," Spalding said to him on several occasions.

I will make you proud, Father, Nox thought. He stepped over the green leaf and continued down the gravel trail. He'd grown accustomed to early-morning walks through the forest over the years. The path he took was his regular one; it was overgrown with vegetation in some spots, and it trailed off the main road. He appreciated the way nature took back the path from man. It gave a sense of peace that the forest continued on after destruction.

The time away from the manor and other people allowed his mind to wander. There were no distractions out here, only nature. Nature reminded him of Lilith as well. His sweet wife who saw him for who he was.

Even after three years, his face had not healed. His slur was still prominent and his face hideously scarred. That didn't matter as much to him anymore. He had Lilith.

Rustling in the forest picked up, piquing Nox's attention. It was probably an animal. He decided to brush it aside. The noise he was making would scare it away.

Nox stepped through some branches that covered the road and came into a clearing where a red-haired girl wearing a skirt held up a partially skinned rabbit with her bloody hand. The other hand gripped a knife that was halfway down the animal. Part of the creature's fur dangled upside down.

The girl looked over at him, her eyes wide in fear. Her face was dirty, youthful too. Her hazelnut eyes, the hair and the age . . . Nox recognized her. The girl he saw at his father's funeral.

"Penny?" Nox said. "Penny . . . Flesher?"

The girl stared at him. Her knife didn't move from the rabbit. About thirty seconds went by before the girl asked, "Who are you?"

"Nox Flesher," he said, taking a slight bow. "Walter's brother."

The girl's arms shook, and she dropped the rabbit with the knife. Her lips trembled slightly before she exploded into a fountain of tears. Penny cried a deathly howl as the water from her eyes washed the mud away from her cheeks. She continued to wail for several minutes.

She'll get it out, Nox thought as he waited. He knew it wouldn't be right to interrupt. He also didn't know how to comfort people with their weird emotions that he didn't understand. He'd do as he always did—let them work through their feelings themselves.

After a good few minutes, the girl wiped her face and sniffled. Her eyes moved back and forth rapidly. "What do I do now?" she asked.

Nox pointed back down the path he'd come from. "You could

stay here, or you can come back to Rutherford Manor with me." *How did she get here?* Nox thought.

Penny looked down at herself, examining the dirt- and blood-covered clothing. Her hair was matted, full of knots and mud. She wiped her hands on her skirt before standing up. "Okay, I'll go with you," she said.

"Al-al-alright," Nox said. "Come."

The girl walked beside Nox, and the two travelled back down the path that he'd come down. Nox took the girl by the hand, and she held it tightly. Bonus point. Nox was learning how to handle emotion. Walking the opposite way on the trail was perplexing for him. On a normal day, Nox would loop around the other way back home, but the routine was out of the question now. How did this wild forest girl wind up on his walking path? Then there was the fact that the forest-girl was his niece. She wasn't much younger than himself, maybe four or five years, tops.

"Wh-wh-what are you doing out here, Penny?" Nox asked.

"I ran," Penny said. She stared forward, not looking at him. The girl seemed traumatized; this wasn't the friendly girl that Nox had seen at the funeral. Something had happened to her.

"Penny, what happened?" Nox asked.

"There was a fire," Penny said. "You're my uncle."

"Yes, Penny, I am. Wh-wh-what was the fire?" Nox asked.

"My home, it burnt down. I don't know what happened. I was out playing after dinner; mom said to be back before dark. I took a nap outside, far longer than I meant to. When I woke, I smelt burning, like a campfire." Penny began to cry again.

Let it out, Nox thought.

Penny cried a little longer until she managed to speak. "I hurried back home. The smell of smoke and fire thickened. When I got back to the house, all I saw were flames. Fire everywhere. The house was covered in it."

"Where was Walter? Or your mother?"

"I couldn't find them, I wanted to get closer to the home and see, but the heat was too much. It was too much. I kn-o-o-ow it was Mu-Mu——!" She began to cry again, muttering the words, making it impossible to hear what she said.

"What?" Nox asked.

The girl continued to cry; she wasn't going to give him anything useful he could work with right now. She was emotionally charged. This was the type of conversation he didn't like to deal with. He'd have to let her exhaust her feelings and talk to her again when she could think clearly.

My brother, Nox thought. He was never fond of how Walter had chosen to leave the family. But he never wanted him to die, either. That marked the second Flesher to perish in an unexplainable manner. The Fleshers' numbers were dwindling fast.

Someone is after us, Nox thought. Sure, three years had passed since his father's death, but to him it seemed too clear not to connect the dots. Maybe he was paranoid. Maybe not. He'd have to discuss this with Lilith and Spalding to get their take on the topic.

Change. Nothing but constant change, Nox thought. Change threw every stable aspect out of balance. It was probably why he enjoyed his walks—they were consistent. But not this time, when his walk brought him in contact with his niece. The niece his brother denied from ever seeing Nox or anyone from Rutherford Manor. Life had changed that.

CHAPTER 22

ALL THINGS COME TO AN END

"You know, Billy," Spalding said, puffing on a smoke, "things haven't really changed much."

Billy took a hit of his tobacco pipe, sitting next to Spalding on the veranda. "How so?"

"I've been thinking . . . I've got some more responsibility now that Alastor is not with us, but it's business as per usual. It certainly helps having you."

"Three years on, and now you discuss this?" Billy asked.

Spalding shrugged. "I don't know. Just random thoughts." Life had actually improved for those of Rutherford Manor.

"We have the butcher shop now," Billy said. "That is a new responsibility."

"Aye," Spalding said. "Jacob really did us a favour with that one. That hasn't built up enough income, though. I was hoping we wouldn't have to keep up this resurrectionist business."

"In time," Billy said.

"Don't remind me," Spalding groaned. "There's still a lot of work that needs to be done to the building, not to mention all the paperwork."

"I'm better at game," Billy said.

"I know where my skills are valued. Don't mean I particularly enjoy it."

Vivian strolled by from around the side of the manor holding a basket full of clean clothes.

"Good afternoon," Spalding said to her.

"Hi, Mr. Savidge!" Vivian said with a smile. "Hi, Billy." She brushed her hair from her face and looked sheepishly down to the ground.

"Vivian." Billy took a slight bow.

The girl hurried inside the manor, holding the basket tightly.

"What was that?" Spalding asked.

"What?" Billy said.

"Vivian blushed all over you, and called you by your first name." Spalding smirked. "Are you two having a pully-hawly?"

"Vivian is a kind girl. Misunderstood, but has a warm heart."

"That she does," Spalding said. "Be careful, though."

"What do you mean?"

"You have nothing to worry about with me, but the folk of Rowley still have issues with. . . ." Spalding paused. "No better way to put this. The blending of cultures."

"Oh." Billy looked to the ground. "I am aware."

"Apologies, friend, I just want to be sure that you and Vivian stay safe."

"We have been meeting in secrecy. We are cautious of what people might say."

"Of course. I'll have your back."

"Thank you," Billy said with a smile. "What of you, Spalding? I have yet to see you with a lady for any longer than a week."

Here we go, Spalding thought. The age-old question that everyone had to ask him about.

A strange surprise worked for Spalding as Nox appeared from his regular walking path. Thanks to the interruption he didn't have to explain—again—to Billy why he wasn't married. Nox was not alone; he had a girl with him.

"Now who the hell is that?" Spalding said, taking a step forward. "Nox has some girl, covered in blood?"

Billy remained silent.

Nox arrived at the veranda with the redheaded girl. She seemed familiar, like from a distant memory.

"Spalding, Billy," Nox said. "W-w-we have a newcomer joining us."

"Hello," Billy said.

"Good afternoon." Spalding tipped his hat at the girl. "Seems like you've had your hands busy," he said.

The girl looked to the ground. She was ashamed. Why?

"This is my niece, P-p-penny Flesher."

Spalding and Billy looked at each other, then at the girl.

Strange, Spalding thought.

"Billy, can you take this girl to Vivian?" Nox said. "Join S-s-spalding and I when you're done. We'll be in the study."

"Of course," Billy said. "Hi Penny, my name is Billy." Billy got up and walked to the door. "Come with me."

Penny's eyes widened as she looked at Nox.

"It's okay," Nox said. "You're safe here."

Penny let go of Nox's hand and strolled towards Billy, following him into the manor.

Nox and Spalding followed behind them and split off into Alastor's old study.

"W-w-we have a situation," Nox said while taking a seat in his reading chair.

"Yeah. That's Walter's girl, right?" Spalding said.

"My b-b-brother is dead," Nox said.

Heavy footsteps came down the hall, and Billy appeared in the entryway.

"Billy," Spalding said.

"What'd I miss?"

"Walter is dead," Spalding said.

"Your brother?" Billy asked, eyeing Nox.

"Y-y-yes," Nox said. "It concerns me. The death has no explanation."

"How did Penny survive?" Spalding asked.

"She said she was outside when a fire occurred at her home. The flames were large, beyond anything a simple accident could cause."

"Thinking it was torched?" Spalding asked.

"M-m-maybe. Penny couldn't find Walter or Lita. It's quite likely they have died."

"Has anyone checked the fire?" Billy asked.

"I b-b-brought Penny back here right away. We could investigate."

"Maybe let the authorities handle that," Spalding said. "They'll make their way here once they know whose home it was."

Nox stared at the ground, his hands curled into fists.

"What's on your mind, Nox?" Spalding asked.

"F-f-first my father, now Walter. That is two Fleshers dead."

"That is over a three-year span," Spalding said.

"Neither death makes any sense," Nox added.

"No, but the Fleshers have always been around the unexplainable. I wouldn't connect the two."

Nox squeezed his fists. "I d-d-don't trust the White Hand."

"Yes, I am aware," Spalding said.

"I've b-b-been giving it some thought. Are you two aware of Bone Bills?"

Billy shook his head.

"They're a part of the Anatomy Act that began in the fifties. I don't know if m-m-my father was aware of them."

"What are they?" Spalding asked.

"The legislation allows anatomists access to unclaimed bodies. When people die, those families that have no money for proper burial leave the bodies."

"So, body donations are legal?" Spalding asked.

"Under th-th-those circumstances, yes. Three out of the five Anatomy Acts have been approved. It won't be long until the other two are. What I-I-I am saying is that the resurrectionist business is on its way out."

"You want to cut ties with the White Hand?" Spalding asked.

"Y-yes I do," Nox said. "We can find better sources of income."

"I hate to say it, but the butcher shop isn't as successful as we had hoped," Spalding said. "It's only been open for two seasons; we just need more time and money with it for the repairs."

Nox nodded. "I am aware. Lilith and I have been working on making new connections in the m-medical industry and the government."

"Government?" Billy asked.

"I f-f-feel my research will offer valuable improvements to the military," Nox said. "We've got arrangements in the works, and we need to clean up our business practices."

Spalding scratched his head. "Might cutting ties with the White Hand be premature until we do finalize those deals?"

"I d-d-don't want the White Hand knowing about what we have. The sooner they are out of the picture, the better."

"We have one more snatch tomorrow," Billy said.

"G-g-good. We end our arrangement then. Provide the body, get payment, and part ways."

Spalding nodded in agreement. The news wasn't what he wanted to hear. Nox was right, though; there wasn't much that could be said about it. Spalding didn't even know about the Bone Bills or the Anatomy Act when he'd started up with Alastor. They were so desperate to make a living that they were willing to dive head-first into the shady business.

All things come to an end, Spalding thought. "What about Penny?" he asked. "If her family is gone, what do we do with her?"

"Sh-sh-she is an adult. She can make her own decisions, but I want to offer to have her stay here with us," Nox said.

"Good call," Spalding said. "There are still plenty of empty rooms at Rutherford Manor."

"I'll t-t-talk to her," Nox said. "See if she has any more insight into her family's death. You two sever our ties with the White Hand."

Spalding nodded. "Deal." He wasn't the biggest fan of the

White Hand either. Their relationship had never fully mended after Blyton's death. Alastor had been far smoother at wooing Bran than Spalding was. Not to mention Spalding never digested the killing well, despite carrying out the acts for years. As it was now, the parties had a one-dimensional relationship with underlying tension. Ending ties with them was probably the best course of action.

CHAPTER 23

TABOO LOVE

The next day Spalding and Billy gathered their resurrectionist tools, loaded up the carriage, and headed out for one last job. Thinking about cutting ties with the White Hand brought all of the flashbacks from three years ago when Spalding and Billy confronted Bran. Oh, how foolish Billy and Spalding had looked in front of the White Hand. Since then, they hadn't had an altercation of such intensity. Spalding hoped dissolving their agreement wouldn't reach that level. This time was different. There was nothing personal involved, and no emotions were attached.

Spalding and Billy exited Rutherford Manor, catching sight of Vivian and Penny sitting on lawn chairs on the veranda. Both girls were having a cup of tea, chitchatting.

"Good luck, you two!" Vivian called out, looking at Billy.

"Thank you," Billy said with a warm smile. Possibly the first friendly smile Spalding had ever seen the man make.

Penny looked at Spalding and gave a closed smiled. He tipped his hat at her.

"She really is wonderful," Billy said.

"You got the honeymoon phase happening," Spalding said.

"I sense skepticism in your tone."

"I've been with enough gals that have been very intriguing, for a little while. Eventually, the mirage wears off and you see them for who they really are. Let me tell you, most of them are bat-shit crazy."

Billy's face squinted. He was offended.

"That is not directed at you or Vivian; she really is a lovely girl. I'm simply explaining the cynicism in my voice."

"You need love in your life, Spalding."

"I get my share." Spalding winked at him.

"Emotional connection. A woman will offer you this. They offer everything a man is incapable of. This is why the two make one. The equal balance."

"Thanks, I'll keep that in mind." *I don't need another lecture about why I need to get married.* Spalding's lack of companionship appeared to be the only constant in his life. Everything else changed for better or worse. This latest change with the White Hand excited him. After all this time, they were finally able to leave this grotesque line of work. Spalding never thought that he'd experience what he'd encountered on the path to attain it, though. Alastor was gone. There were new faces at Rutherford Manor. The butcher shop was not as glorious as he'd hoped. One thing was certain, though: his sense of right and wrong would be put to rest. Finally.

"I never did get used to this," Spalding said as the carriage rode into town.

"Snatching?" Billy said.

"Killing I've always been fine with. Cleaning up the dirty work of the Fleshers has always been a part of my job. I don't mind that. What bugs me is the hunting and preying on people. That hits me the wrong way, you know?"

"I see," Billy said. His tone made it clear he didn't understand. Spalding knew Billy was pleased as long as he was able to feed his craving for violence.

"I will miss it," Billy said. "What will I do? I need this."

"We can still throw some fists around at the fight club," Spalding said. "Plus, we need your skills for game meat."

"True. But I fear that might not be enough to keep the darkness at bay."

Spalding scratched his head. He knew Billy was troubled, but sometimes he wanted to tell the man to snap out of it. Addictions could be beaten. Of course, that was assuming it was just an addiction. Billy seemed so convinced that his tale of a demon possessing his mother's womb was real. Crazy.

"We'll keep you busy," Spalding said. "Rutherford Manor has many moving parts; I wouldn't worry about it."

The two men arrived in Chicago, parked the carriage, and continued on to scope out potential targets. Spalding was actually eager to find the new, and final, target so they could just be done with it. Never before had he been so willing to partake in a snatch other than today. Some poor soul would be the casualty of this final deal. Too bad for them. Too bad for the countless other people throughout the years.

Spalding and Billy leaned against a brick wall, each smoking a cigarette, watching the busy crowd of the marketplace. It was the same market that Spalding and Alastor had visited on the second snatch. The location created a sense of déjà vu and loathing inside of Spalding. He missed Alastor. It was a simple as that. Sure, he had learned to move on, but the sorrow never left. The lack of answers to the man's death was a constant burn.

"What about that one?" Billy asked, pointing at a dark-haired man in the marketplace.

Spalding eyed the man closer. The long dark hair and thin frame made his identity obvious: Niles. "Wait," Spalding said, suddenly standing up straight. "The thin, pasty fellow?"

"Yes."

"Billy, that is Niles."

"No way, Niles doesn't have a kid."

A group of old ladies moved out of Spalding's view, revealing a boy beside the presumed Niles. The dark-haired boy looked up at the man, exposing a scar that ran down his face.

No, Spalding thought. It couldn't be, could it? It was like looking at a ghost of the past. The scar, the hair, approximately the right age: the boy from the Black Hand family. He stood only half a dozen meters away.

A flash of the snatch went through Spalding's mind. Alastor and Spalding had entered the Black Hand family's home that fateful night and cruelly slain the boy's mother and father. Well, the husband. Seeing Niles today, it became clear he may be the real father. Irene's threat to Niles the night she and Spalding spent together supported the theory.

We killed Niles' lover, Spalding thought. It explained why the man was so in the dumps after that second snatch. The boy survived. Niles was miserable. Could the boy have identified Alastor and Spalding to Niles? It wasn't a farfetched hunch.

The dark-haired man turned to face the boy with a smile, and he handed the kid a fruit. The elongated nose and brown eyes were, without a doubt, Niles. Spalding suddenly realized there may be truth to his speculations.

"Huh," Billy said. "That is Niles."

"Billy," Spalding said. "This could be big. Let's keep an eye on them."

"What do you suppose this is?" Billy said.

"Remember the fiasco I told you about? With Niles having a Black Hand lover?"

"Yes," Billy said.

"That kid is the one that got away when Alastor and I killed his parents."

"I see. What do you propose?"

"I'm not sure. That kid could have described us to Niles. Maybe they have some sort of info on Alastor's death." He looked up at the sky; it wasn't much past late afternoon. "We have time before the snatch. Let's see what these two do." *Maybe there's something here,* Spalding thought. He was purely basing his guess on his gut feeling. Niles was a man of secrets. Spalding and Alastor had murdered his lover. There had to be a connection.

The two men watched Niles and the boy from afar, following as they moved throughout the marketplace for about an hour, just before dusk.

As the marketplace cleared, Niles gave the boy a big hug and then waved goodbye to him. He had to be going to the White Hand, prepping to meet Spalding and Billy. The boy went the opposite direction, off into the side streets.

"Okay, follow the boy," Spalding said. "Let's see if we can get some answers to all of this."

The two marched on the opposite side of the street, following the kid as he walked past some homes. There were still a lot of people out and about, which would make an interrogation a challenge.

"There are too many people," Spalding said. "We need more cover."

"I got an idea," Billy said. "Let me circle around, approach him from the front. I'll introduce him to my knife."

"Don't stab him," Spalding said.

"No, just a threat."

"Okay." Spalding looked at the boy, who walked with little care. He had no idea that the man who murdered his family was right behind him. This was why Spalding hated killing: the aftermath. It was never pleasant.

"Billy, you take this one. I don't need that kid seeing me." Spalding knew the boy might recognize him. He didn't need the kid whining to Niles about their interaction.

"Understood." Billy sped up his walk, crossing the street and heading around the corner.

Spalding continued to follow the boy from the other side of the road. *Don't look back, kid,* Spalding thought. As long as he kept his distance, even if the kid did look back, he was in the clear.

Billy re-emerged from around the corner at the end of the block. He walked past a group of elderly people, then a lady, and then finally the boy. The kid tried to move around Billy, who stepped in front of him again. Billy pulled his coat open, revealing his knife. His lips moved, but Spalding couldn't hear.

The boy took a step back, and Billy took one forward. Billy said something. A statement that caused the boy to stand still. The kid put his hands in his pockets, and the two chatted for several minutes. Then, the kid attempted to make a dash.

Billy snagged the kid by the collar of his coat, lifting him off the ground.

Be easy, Billy, Spalding thought.

The boy squirmed for a moment but relaxed. "Okay!" he shouted.

The shout caught the attention of some passersby, who glanced over for a moment before continuing on with their walk. Close call. The kid calmed down, and Billy put him down on the ground. They chatted for a few more minutes until Billy tipped his hat and walked passed the boy. The kid glanced back.

Shit, Spalding pulled his hat down to cover his face.

Billy crossed the street. "That was the boy," he said.

"Great," Spalding said. He lifted his hat to see the boy had turned away and walked out of sight. "What else did he have to say?"

"He's a smart kid. His name is Arnaldo. He knows about his mother's affair with Niles, his father."

"So, Niles took him in?"

"Not quite. Angeline, his mother, was married to Donnie, the Black Hand mobster. Donnie never suspected that Arnaldo was not his kid."

Spalding folded his arms. "So when the kid ran away, he went to Niles. He had to have told Niles what we looked like."

"Possibly. I asked him if he knew who killed his family. The boy said he didn't know. I didn't want to interrogate him too long. The chat was getting people's attention."

"Of course," Spalding said. "But we should tell Nox about this."

"Yes. Do we talk to Niles?"

"We will. Let's do this job first, then discuss with Nox." *Ghosts of the past,* Spalding thought. It seemed Nox wasn't wrong about the White Hand being involved with Alastor's death after all.

CHAPTER 24

JUST BUSINESS

Target. Stalk. Attack. Kill. Wrap up. The regular old routine of the resurrectionist business, except with a twist of murder. This was an extraordinary catch; they would never have to do this process again. Hearing the poor man's scream and gurgle as Billy choked the life out of him was the most satisfying sound Spalding had ever heard, even down to the last gasp for air before the man passed on. Pierre was also able to witness the event. Spalding had had enough time to take the cane out of the carriage as he watched the man's end near. The death was the mark of a new era. A long-awaited one.

Spalding and Billy got out of Chicago and hurried over to the regular meeting spot, waiting for the White Hand to arrive. Spalding's hands were sweaty. They rarely were. He always had a handle on his emotions. But ending the snatching gig was too desirable an idea not to be nervous about it.

Three horses trotted up the hill and into the lantern light

of the carriage. Bran, Niles, and Irene. They never did replace Blyton, the poor bloke that attempted to take on Billy.

"Spalding," Bran said while hopping off his horse. He tipped his hat. "Good evening."

Spalding returned the gesture. "Evening."

Niles and Irene dismounted as well. The girl glared at Spalding, as she did every meetup. She was probably still mad that he broke her nose. The cartilage never did heal the same. Spalding found the slight angle was actually an attractive feature. That didn't help his lust for her. Maybe the pistol whip had done more damage to him than it did her.

"What do you have for us today?" Bran asked.

"Oh, this is just a chum. Not much special about him," Spalding said.

"Good as any," Bran replied.

The group walked to the back of the carriage as Billy unlocked the door.

Niles stood beside Spalding. The man whom Angeline had loved enough to have a secret child with. Angeline, the dead woman. Had Niles murdered Alastor for revenge?

Let's see what we can dig up, Spalding thought. "Hey, Niles," Spalding said.

"Yeah?" Niles replied, not looking at him.

"I'm getting married. Any advice?"

"Why would I have advice? I'm not married."

"Oh, right, that was just your lover. Apologies. Time has a funny way of scrambling my memory."

"Aye," Niles said, squinting. He seemed more confused than anything. A fruitless attempt.

Billy popped open the back of the carriage and stepped aside for Irene and Bran to look at the body.

Spalding leaned closer to Niles. "Never found yourself a new gal?" he asked.

"No. I see you've gotten over your bachelor life. Congratulations. What's her name?"

"Jenny," Spalding lied.

"Lovely name," Niles replied.

"Thanks. I hope you find a lady to marry and settle down with a son."

Niles looked down to the ground, saying nothing.

Gotcha, Spalding thought. Seeing the man look down mirrored the time when Spalding confronted Bran all those years ago. Niles had looked down as Irene took the lead. Niles knew something. The man also had nothing to say to Spalding a week later. Why did he not answer him now? Because he already had a son. His boss, Bran, couldn't know. Irene, maybe. She knew about the affair.

"Perfect," Bran said. "Irene, Niles," he ordered. That was enough for them to know what to do. This was routine.

Bran and Spalding walked together back to the horses where Bran got the cash bag from his horse's saddle.

"All there," Bran said, handing Spalding the bag.

"Thank you." Spalding extended his hand.

Bran looked confused. They never shook hands. "What is this?" Bran asked. "You better not be trying anything stupid. I haven't forgotten."

"No, not like that all. I'm shaking your hand to respect the fact that you've continued to work with us over the years."

Bran nodded and shook Spalding's hand with a firm grip. "Likewise. Overall we've had a fairly good arrangement."

"About that," Spalding said while letting go. "We've had a discussion about the resurrectionist business. You're aware of the Bone Bills, and the Anatomy Acts, right?"

"Yeah, I've heard of it," Bran said. "That was almost half a century ago, and it hasn't taken effect in Illinois."

"Well, three of the acts are approved. This isn't a sustainable business model."

"It's been fine so far," Bran said.

"The need for bodies is going to start to dwindle, so we're getting out of it while we're ahead."

"Really? Whose idea was that, Nox's?" Bran asked.

"He learned of the legislation, and I agree with him."

Irene and Niles walked by the two of them. Irene and Spalding locked eyes for a moment before he looked away. "Truthfully, I have never been fond of this kind of work and am looking forward to getting out of it."

Bran nodded. "Yeah, you never seemed to care for it much. You don't have a lot to lose, either."

"No, I'd personally rather do something with a little more authenticity. Build something worth losing."

Bran smirked. "Okay, what will you do?" Bran asked.

"Start up a butcher shop, who knows."

"Fair enough. Now I gotta replace you two goons." Bran said with a smile. "You really are good at pissing me off."

Spalding smirked. "That seems to be a skill of mine."

Bran tipped his hat and returned to his horse, mounting it. Before he turned to leave, he said, "Spalding."

"Yes?"

"If you ever tire of Alastor's boy's immaturity, come find me."

Spalding took a slight bow. "I'll keep that in mind."

The White Hand members' horses galloped away. Irene was the last to leave, blowing a kiss to Spalding before riding off into the night. The girl who he couldn't get out of his head. The gal who denied any advances Spalding made after their night of passion. She called the shots. Not him.

Spalding's spine tingled. *Not a chance,* he thought. Having Irene more prominent in his world, only to taunt him, was not his idea of a simple life.

CHAPTER 25

PREP TIME

Billy and Spalding returned to Rutherford Manor that night, as they did after every snatch. Thankfully, this was the last night going back and forth from Chicago. They were finished. Spalding was relieved. But unfortunately, more alarming news had arrived with the discovery of Arnaldo and Niles.

Spalding thought about how he could approach the situation with Nox. What would be the best way, so the kid didn't throw a fit like he usually did when something involved emotions? Lilith marrying him, and his father's death had given him a metaphoric kick in the ass to grow up, just not enough. At the same time, the boy still had a hard time accepting the greyer areas of life. His father's death being unsolved was one of them.

Their carriage arrived late in the night as usual. At this point in time, everyone was asleep. They'd have to bring up the discovery of Arnaldo with Nox tomorrow.

"Catch you in the morning," Spalding said to Billy as they

parted ways in the foyer. Billy's room was on the main floor, while Spalding's was up on the second level.

"Goodnight," Billy said while leaving down the hall.

Before Spalding took the first step up the stairs, a squeaky voice came from the living room. "Do you always get home so late?"

Spalding turned to see that a girl sat in a chair. The voice and size of the girl made it clear it was Penny.

"What are you doing in the dark?" Spalding asked.

"I can't sleep," she said.

Spalding pulled out a match from his pocket and lit it, walking to the candle at the entryway dresser. He took the flame and walked into the living room, casting the dim light over the scene. Penny sat in the chair. Her eyes were heavy and her face sad.

"Can't sleep?" Spalding asked.

"No," the girl repeated, watching him.

Spalding sat down across from her. "What's on your mind?"

Penny looked to the ground. "I never sleep well. Mun is always around."

"Mun?"

"Muunat. She's an owl that has never been very nice to me. She was pecking at the window tonight."

That name, Spalding thought. He'd heard it before from Billy. The demon. How did a Flesher know of the same demon as Billy's mother? *Billy, telling campfire tales to little girls,* he thought. It'd be best to try and help Penny get some sleep. "It's just an animal. Shoo it away."

"She's not like other animals."

"Well, I can assure you that she isn't one to worry about," Spalding said. "Anything else?"

"The sheriff came by today about the fire."

"Oh?" Spalding said. "What did he have to say?"

"The fire was an accident. They think my mother or father might have made a mistake. Cooking or something."

"That seems odd. What do you think?" Spalding asked.

"I think Muunat had something to do with it."

"Is Billy telling you scary stories?"

Penny began to play with her hair. "No." She looked at him and smiled weakly. "So, you work with my uncle?"

"Aye, we began to work together after his father passed. You were at his funeral."

"I remember," Penny said. "You were there. Always funny."

"I'm a real jokester." Spalding looked up to the second floor. "I've been out all night and need to get some rest. Don't stay up too late." He got up, placed the candle on the coffee table, and exited the room.

"Spalding," Penny called out.

"Yes?" Spalding asked.

"Thank you."

"For what?"

"Talking. It's nice to talk."

"Yeah, goodnight." Spalding left the room. *Strange girl,* he thought. It made sense; she was a Flesher. None of them were of the typical type. It was probably why the Savidges stuck around. There was never a dull moment.

Shame she isn't a bit older, Spalding thought. She might be odd, but so was he. The girl was also familiar with how Rutherford

Manor functioned. From what Spalding had seen when first meeting Penny, with her bloody hands, she was no stranger to the gory and the obscure. Something most gals wouldn't be able to come to terms with.

Spalding made it to his room and fell asleep instantly. It was possibly one of the best sleeps he'd had in years. There were no worries about the resurrection business ever again. He didn't have to be concerned about finding the next catch, or making sure that they were careful with who they killed. There was no concern of destroying any evidence. He always wondered if the law would eventually find them. They never did . . . so far. The Fleshers and Savidges had been cunning over the many decades they'd collaborated. He'd just hate to be the one that messed it all up.

The next morning Spalding woke. He had slept long past sunrise; that was abnormal for him. He was usually an early riser and late sleeper. Guess there really was some weight lifted off his shoulders after closing up shop with the White Hand.

He got dressed, washed up, and hurried down to the main floor.

Okay, time to get Nox in on this, Spalding thought.

He went to Nox's study to find the youngest Flesher son was nowhere to be seen. The boy was probably in his torture-dungeon of a basement. Correction—'his laboratory,' as Nox called it. Spalding didn't know the difference. He only heard screams of pain echoing down there.

Spalding went down to the basement level with a lantern to make it through the darker halls. The back room was lit up. Someone was here.

A muffled groan could be heard from the room, the sound bouncing off the walls of the hallway. Nox was up to something.

Spalding entered the room to see a man on an operating table, chained down. His stomach was cut open as he breathed rapidly. A man in a bloody shirt and apron stood over him with a needle in hand.

"Nox," Spalding said.

Nox turned around; he had an operating cap and goggle-infused mask on. The cover had a grill filter for the mouth and was made of thick leather.

"Christ, Nox, what the hell is that?"

He lifted the mask with his free hand, revealing his half-scarred face. "L-l-lilith made it for me."

"I've never seen you wear that hideous thing," Spalding said.

"I've had it for a while. It helps keep the fumes out of my face."

"As you inject these people with unknown dope," Spalding said, walking up to the operating table.

Nox pulled his mask back down. "Y-y-yes. In simple terms. Careful," he said, his voice muffled from the mask. "The fumes are toxic."

"What is this?" Spalding asked. The man on the table was wide-eyed, looking at Spalding. He tried to talk, but only gurgles came out of his mouth. He was oddly energetic for a man that had his guts on the table.

Nox took the syringe and injected it into the man's neck. "This is an improvement from th-th-the solution Lilith and I made for you and my father. It paralyzes them. It keeps them awake, reduces pain—only slightly—and decreases their reception to shock. They experience every moment just as conscious as you or I do right now, without any of their nervous system warning them of their dismembered body."

"Intriguing. Why?"

"Surgery, for one," Nox said. "Torture is another. Experimentation on living samples is a third."

"You always loved your live samples," Spalding said. "We need to talk."

"P-p-please talk," Nox said while grabbing some surgical tools.

Spalding pointed at the man on the table. "Can he hear us?"

"Yes," Nox said as he dug the tools into the open gut of the man.

"Is he going to be around much longer?"

"Probably not."

"Okay. Billy and I went into town and ended our relations with the White Hand. We are in the clear for that; no more body snatching."

"Excellent, that is wonderful news," Nox said.

"Yes, it is wonderful news. Believe me, I am beyond thrilled to be finished with that business."

"How did Bran take it?"

"Bran took it fine." Spalding paused. *Here we go, let's break the news.* "Did I ever tell you about the second snatching your father and I did?"

"No, I c-c-can't say you have."

"We invaded the home of a wealthy family, killing the mother and father. Their son witnessed the crime and got away. Later we found out that they were members of the Black Hand—the

Italian gangsters. Nothing came of it, or so we thought. But last night Billy and I ran into a boy—the same boy from all those years ago. He was with Niles."

"Niles? The name is familiar. You've mentioned him."

"Yes. I caught wind Niles had a secret lover, a married woman of the Black Hand. The dots connect, and the boy is Niles's kid."

"This boy—he escaped from you and my father?"

"He did. He saw our faces. He's with Niles now, his real father."

Nox froze, his hands still in the man's stomach. "W-w-wait. Niles is a member of the White Hand?"

"Aye. Your father and I didn't know at the time but we killed his lover, Angeline."

"And his boy?"

"Arnaldo. He saw us and went to Niles."

"Is it a f-f-far leap for me to accuse him? For killing my father?"

"The boy was probably too young," Spalding said. "We haven't confronted Niles, though. It is a good hypothesis, and I think we should see what we can dig up. He has a guilty face; I know one when I see one."

"Wh-wh-where is Niles now?" Nox asked, pulling his hands out of the man's stomach. Blood dripped from his tools.

"Not sure. He comes to the fight club frequently."

Nox dropped his dirty tools on the tray and lifted his mask. "I need to join you."

"You're not exactly cut out for the fight club, no offence," Spalding said. "How about I talk to him?"

"N-n-no. I must be involved this time. I'm not looking to fight. We just follow Niles until we get him alone."

Nox was stubborn, like Alastor. The young Flesher was upset about his father's death, and rightfully so. Spalding could argue with him how he had no place going to the fight club since he couldn't brawl. There wasn't going to be much convincing him, though; once his mind was made up, he was on a one-way ticket. Another trait he shared with Alastor.

"Alright," Spalding said. "We'll take you to the fight club. We'll confront Niles. You might be challenged to a dance—just a warning."

"Y-y-yes. Whe-when is the fight club?" Nox asked.

"In the next couple of days," Spalding said.

A wicked smile grew on the undamaged side of Niles's face. He grabbed the surgical knife from the table and then plunged it into the neck of the man on the table. The man didn't yelp or scream. His eyes didn't even react to the stabbing. Instead, he looked around the room, confused, then down at his open organs. He tried to speak but groaned some more as his eyelids began to sag until they covered his eyes completely. A discombobulating death. A cruel, unnatural one. One that could only be experienced through the hands of a Flesher.

CHAPTER 26

FIST FULL OF VENGEANCE

Two days passed. Two long days of anticipation, waiting to go and confront the man who could have insight into what happened to Nox's father. Nox was calculative in nature and didn't jump recklessly into action. But this time, he couldn't wait. He didn't want to let Spalding do the heavy work for him. He regretted not being there to confront Bran about Alastor's death and wasn't going to make the same mistake this time. If Niles really was the man who was responsible for his father's demise, he had to see it through himself. The only issue Nox had with going to the fight club was that he did not know how to fight.

Spalding and Billy gave him a few basic lessons, showing him how to block and how to punch. They shared a few cheap tactics to give him the upper hand. They also warned him what to look out for in an opponent. Both Billy and Spalding had a few trial brawls with Nox which ended with the Flesher boy on his ass.

Fighting was a lot more work than Nox had first anticipated.

"You'll learn quickly," Spalding said as he extended a hand to Nox, who sat on the grass after Spalding's finishing kick.

Nox took Spalding's offered hand and wiped the sweat from his face. That was their last go before they headed into Rowley. He felt his heart race from anticipation for the night ahead.

Lilith gave Nox a kiss on the cheek and a tight hug as he prepared to leave for the night. She slipped a small, spiky band into his hand. It was sized to fit around his finger.

"What's this?" Nox asked.

"It's a poison. It will disorient your target. Just don't stab yourself with it. That should give you the upper hand you need."

Nox nodded. "Th-th-thank you."

Lilith gave him a gentle kiss on his lips, saying farewell before she stepped aside. Vivian and Penny waved goodbye as well, watching the three men leave the manor.

"Let's get going," Spalding said as he glanced at Penny before turning to face the door.

Nox noted the interaction. It was the second such incident he'd observed. Only a few days ago, he overheard Penny and Spalding talking when he returned from the last trip into Chicago. Nox often worked late and the flooring wasn't very thick. You could hear quite a bit from the basement of Rutherford Manor.

Nox followed Billy and Spalding out the door. Nox rode on the back of Spalding's horse; they only ever had two animals, as any more got to be pretty expensive. He held on to Spalding so he wouldn't fall off as they rode into town.

"Anything else I should kn-know about this fight club?" Nox

asked.

"Well, don't get emotional. You're pretty good at that, though," Spalding said with a smirk.

Nox rolled his eyes. He knew the humour; it was the same type of statement that Spalding made often throughout the years. He got it; he didn't have any feelings. The joke was old now.

"Spalding," Nox said.

"Yeah?" Spalding replied.

"H-h-have you thought about marriage?"

"You too?" Spalding laughed. "Now I think everyone has asked me about this. Why you of all people?"

"B-b-because of Penny. My niece. She needs a good man."

Spalding remained silent for several moments. "I didn't expect to hear such words from you. You'll make a good father."

"Th-thanks. I'm simply putting the word out there. Penny is a Flesher; we are loyal and strong, as you know. Penny seems to take kindly to you as well. She's all on her own, too."

"Thank you, Nox. I'll keep the thought in mind."

Despite his exterior behaviour, Nox had a good heart. He just had trouble expressing his emotions. He wanted Spalding to be happy, and he wanted his niece to have a good life. He'd said what he could; the rest was up to Spalding.

The three rode into the outskirts of Rowley. From what Spalding had said, the fight club took place at various locations in the surrounding area. This edition of the event happened to be in town, at an old inn.

Spalding and Billy tied the horses to a post and walked to the building. Nox couldn't help but admire their relaxed and casual stroll. Going to a secret location to throw fists into people's faces was their hobby, their pastime. Nox didn't understand why or how. What made this type of behaviour so appealing to men? It served no purpose and brought no progress. Yet, they walked with far more confidence than Nox had ever had.

"Remember, Nox," Spalding said. "You fight if someone challenges you."

"Remind me why?" Nox asked.

"Respect. You'll look like a coward, and it will look bad upon Billy and I. This place is sort of invite-only; it's not a free for all."

"Understood," Nox said.

The three entered the building. Lights were on. A teller was at the front desk but paid no attention to them. Cheers erupted from a staircase leading to the lower level. The fight club was obviously down there.

The three men descended the creaky steps to the basement. The air was warm, humid, and had a smoky haze of cigarette smoke. Some groups of onlookers were clumped together in bunches, watching men slam fists into each other. Other groups were farther back, some in a line and others in more casual stances.

Spalding pointed at the men in a line. "Only talk to them if you're looking to brawl," he said.

"Got you," Nox said.

Billy patted Nox on the shoulder. "Tonight, you will taste blood."

"I h-h-have. Not intentionally, but I have."

Billy chuckled. "No, you haven't."

Nox swallowed heavily. Billy's words weren't exactly

reassuring. Was he making a mistake coming here? The constant shouting, the thick haze, the smells. He began to feel claustrophobic from the condensed space and tight air. No. He couldn't let his senses overstimulate him. This was the closest he had ever been to finding out any information about his father. He couldn't give up.

Billy turned to the group, stopping in his tracks. "We're here, so I am going to participate."

"Be my guest," Spalding said. "I need a drink."

Billy wandered off into the crowd and Spalding began to stray off to the far back of the basement where the casual conversations happened. Some kegs were stacked in the back of the room. Nox didn't want to be left behind. Following Billy seemed weird since he was off to fight. Spalding was the best bet. He picked up his pace to catch up with the man. The two stopped at the bar, and Spalding handed some cash over the counter, ordering a drink.

"You want anything?" Spalding asked, looking at Nox.

"N-n-no, I am fine, thanks," Nox said.

Spalding got his drink from the bartender and took a big gulp. "I gotta say, you have some balls for coming out here."

"Th-thank you."

"Or you're really that blinded by your anger."

Nox looked at him. "Sorry?"

"I get why you're so upset that your father died. It wasn't the right time, and you were thrown to the wolves, taking care of your family."

Nox folded his arms. "I w-w-was ready," he said, trying to convince himself. He knew damn well that it was a lie. Fear overran him daily.

"You're not fooling me, Nox," Spalding said. "We've known each other long enough that simply saying you aren't afraid isn't going to work on me."

"Alright, I am scared. How c-c-can I not be?"

"Not saying you shouldn't be. Just don't let it cloud your judgement too much," Spalding said.

They rested against the bar and watched the fights. A few people that walked by did a double-take at Nox and his scarred face. That was the usual reaction he got. The few times he did go out people always gave a long stare to confirm to themselves that he really did have half a face. This was his reality.

They spotted Billy in one of the rings, having a go with a brawny, bearded man. The fight was quick, over in a few swings. Billy threw one fist to the jaw that spun the man around and sent him to the floor. The crowd cheered with excitement.

"He sure has a lot to let out," Spalding said with a chuckle.

Spalding was enjoying this? Nox couldn't possibly see why. All he could see were a bunch of animals making noise.

Billy left the ring and wandered to the back, where he found Nox and Spalding. He wiped his face of sweat and let out a sigh of satisfaction.

"Good show," Spalding said.

"His spirit had too much fire," Billy said.

The three watched as the people continued to fight, take bets and mingle. To Nox, time seemed to crawl by. He knew roughly what Niles looked like but was relying on Spalding and Billy to spot him. Niles had to be here.

"When d-d-does he normally arrive?" Nox asked.

Spalding shrugged. "Niles? He isn't here all the time. When he is, he gets here before me."

"Look," Billy said, nodding his head to the staircase.

Nox and Spalding glanced over to see that a dark-haired man had arrived. He dressed clean, with a vest and dress pants. He held his hat in his hand and was accompanied by a woman who dressed oddly like a man. Nox rarely saw a woman in pants, a blouse and a vest like this one.

"Great," Spalding muttered while taking a gulp of his drink. "I was hoping she wouldn't show."

"Who is that?" Nox asked.

"That would be Irene," Billy said. "Spalding fucked her."

"Not everyone needs to know," Spalding said.

Billy chuckled.

"L-l-let's confront him," Nox said.

"No, we'll play it cool. Especially with the two of them here." Spalding stood up from the bar. "I'll go talk to him. You two stay here."

"I w-w-want to join," Nox said. He hadn't come this far just to stand in the back and watch. He had to be part of every moment.

"Stay calm," Spalding said. "Don't worry, I'll introduce you." He turned around and pursued Niles and Irene.

"Breathe through your nose," Billy said.

Nox looked up at him. "S-s-sorry?"

"Breathe through your nose, out your mouth. It will help center you."

Nox hadn't even noticed he was breathing rapidly. His anger was beginning to boil. He paused his breath and followed Billy's instructions. Nox took deep breaths through his nose and out his mouth, focusing on the air that entered and exited his lungs. The slight distraction was helpful as he watched Spalding chit-chat with Niles and Irene. The woman seemed to stare at him with eagle-like eyes. She never blinked. It was like a bizarre mixture of anger and magnetism.

"Wud-appened tuh yer face?" came a man's voice as spit flew into Nox's ear.

Don't be talking to me, Nox thought. He knew that couldn't possibly be the case. Saliva was on his skin, and who else had a face like his?

"Aye!" came the voice as someone tapped his shoulder.

Nox looked over to see a man who stared at him with one eye half open. He reeked of piss and alcohol.

"Aye, sorry lad!" he said. "Just noticed yer face."

"An ac-ac-accident," Nox said.

"Well, I th-th-think we need tuh rumble it out. That might make ye feel better. Wuddayah say?"

Nox looked over at Spalding, who was still chatting with the White Hand, then at Billy, who stared at him, saying nothing.

"Okay," Nox said. "We'll f-f-fight." He fiddled with his hands, feeling the band that wrapped around his index finger. He still had Lilith's poison. The room was dark. As long as he kept his hand out of sight, he could sneak a jab in.

This is crazy, Nox thought as he felt his stomach twist from his nerves. He was a man of science, reason, and logic. Fighting didn't align with any of those values. That didn't matter now. He was in the thick of it, and there wasn't much he could do.

"Ah-right, splendid!" the man said. "There's ah free ring

over'ere. Winner gets a buck?" The man turned and started walking away, presuming that Nox was following.

For my father, Nox thought while clenching his fists.

"Here," Billy said while extending his hand. "Get rid of your coat. The vest too."

"Wh-wh-why?" Nox asked.

"You'll be able to move better."

Nox surrendered his coat and unbuttoned his vest, passing it to Billy. He rolled up his sleeves as well before catching up to the man that challenged him. The man was oddly well balanced in his walk for being as drunk as he was.

"I didn't catch yah name, lad?" said the drunk. "I'm Arnold."

"Nox," Nox said.

"Lovely name," said Arnold as he made his way into the ring.

Nox followed, and the two men in the ring quickly caught the attention of nearby watchers, who fluttered around like pigeons waiting to eat, hungry for a show.

"Yeh eveah done one o'these? I haven't seen yeh before," Arnold asked while raising his hands.

"Not here," Nox said, bringing up his own fists. It felt so unnatural to be in such a stance. Then there was the crowd around him. He could feel his heart rate increase and his body begin to sweat uncontrollably.

Arnold stepped forward and lunged at him with a fist. Nox was able to dodge the attack. The man was sloppy in his movements, swaying slightly from his liquor but he still kept his balance. He swung again, this time hitting Nox in the shoulder.

The blow had a lot more impact than he expected and threw him off-center. He recovered and stepped back. The two men circled around each other for a moment before Arnold attacked again; this was a wide swing. There was an opening at his torso. Nox could strike.

Nox let out a roar and lunged his band-fingered fist forward. The blow hit the man in the chest, the ring pricking his skin. The collision threw Arnold backwards slightly. Nox didn't realize how much another man weighed and how little his fist would impact someone. The blow also hurt his wrist.

Arnold recovered and smiled. "Good hit!" His face quickly went grim, and he licked his lips. He swayed slightly and tumbled once before regaining balance.

"You alright?" Nox asked. He couldn't tell if the man was that drunk or the poison was beginning to kick in.

"Yeh, just a bit too much tah drink," Arnold said. He raised his fists up again and began closing in on Nox.

Nox held his fists up, feeling confident after his first successful punch. His heart raced as sweat drizzled down his face. His body heat increased like he had never experienced before. This was an adrenaline rush. He went on the offence, throwing another jab at the man with his non-band hand. The blow hit Arnold in the face. The man didn't even move. Perhaps the poison was working.

Nox hit him again, and again! Blood pumped through his body as his heart beat faster. Nox sent one last blow towards Arnold, and the man met the ground. The crowd laughed, clapped, and cheered.

Laughing? Nox thought. *But I won! Is this funny?* He was confused as to why some people were finding this amusing. Then it hit him: On some sick level, people enjoyed watching the violence. It was similar to Nox's obsession with opening people up to see how their internal organs worked.

Nox stepped out of the ring, confused and unsure how to end it. He looked back to see Arnold wave his limbs around a bit trying to get up, but ultimately lay down on the ground.

"Well done," Spalding's voice came out. "You defeated a drunk!"

Nox turned to see Spalding was with Billy at the edge of the crowd. "Wh-wh-why are people laughing?"

"Because you beat up a sloshed fool," Billy said. "It's funny." He handed Nox his vest and coat.

"I s-s-suppose so," Nox said, putting on his coat and vest. He looked around trying to spot Niles. "Where is Niles?"

"He's here," Spalding said. "Just back in the corner there. We'll keep watch on him."

Nox looked over to where Spalding pointed. Niles was at the far end of the room with the girl named Irene. He stared at Niles. Nox's whole body vibrated with violent energy—a new kind of energy he wasn't used to. It was powerful. Enjoyable. Maybe there was something to the fight club after all.

He fiddled in his coat pocket, feeling the syringe. *You're next.*

CHAPTER 27

FINALE

Why'd she have to be here? That was the question that ran through Spalding's mind throughout the night. He should have expected it. She was almost always at the fight club when Niles was here. They seemed to think they could bring on more goons for the White Hand by recruiting in Rowley. But Spalding never saw them have any luck.

Even walking up and talking to Irene and Niles irritated him. Why couldn't they get out of his life? Irene was like a fly that wouldn't go away. And her presence here made the plan to confront Niles a bit more challenging.

"I'll have to keep Irene busy," Spalding said to Billy and Nox. "She and Niles are rarely apart, and when they leave, they'll leave together."

"Fair enough," Billy said. "Should we really be worried? This will be easy."

"Aye," Spalding said, taking a chug of his drink. "Just clarifying.

271

Irene is Bran's daughter, after all." *Nothing to do with how that gal rattles me up. Not at all.* He didn't like being nervous. Would they have to kill Irene? If Niles really was the one behind this, they didn't need a witness for what they were about to do. Especially a witness who was the daughter of the White Hand boss.

"We'll knock her out," Billy said. "She won't know anything."

Spalding looked over at Nox, who was not paying attention to the conversation. He gazed off to the far corner where Irene and Niles stood. His fists were coiled, shaking.

"Nox, your fight's over," Spalding said.

Nox snapped out of his trance and looked over. "S-s-sorry?" he asked.

"We were just discussing our game plan. You and Billy can handle Niles. I'll distract Irene, presuming she joins Niles when he leaves."

"G-g-got it," Nox said.

The three watched as the night carried on. Outside of their scheme to confront Niles, the rest of the night was a regular fight club. Spalding and Billy participated in some fights and Nox did his best to avoid any interaction with anyone. He did well. He didn't have to partake in any more matches after defeating the drunk.

The numbers in the crowd began to dwindle as the night progressed. Spalding was a few drinks in. He felt his tension regarding Irene start to diminish. Liquid courage was always a solid solution. It sure helped suppress his thoughts of what the three of them were waiting to do to Niles and Irene.

The three kept their spot at the back of the room by the bar. Nox rarely moved from the location while Spalding and Billy socialized and watched some of the fights. Nox noticed Niles and Irene also were sociable during the night. They crossed paths a couple of times and commented about the fights. It was friendly behaviour.

There we are, Spalding thought, watching as Niles and Irene finally began to make their way to the staircase leading to the main floor.

"Billy, Nox," Spalding said. "This might be it."

Nox's eyes widened as he locked his gaze on the two White Hand members. The rate of his breathing increased.

That kid really has a lot of pent-up energy, Spalding thought. *Fighting on a regular basis might actually help him out.*

Niles and Irene reached the staircase and disappeared up to the main floor.

"That's it," Spalding said while lifting his pint glass to his mouth and tipping his head back, pouring all of the beer down his throat. He wiped his face and exhaled. "Game time."

The three men gathered their belongings and hurried out of the basement, going up to the main floor of the hotel. Niles and Irene were nowhere to be seen; they must have already gone out the entrance.

Exiting the hotel, the group spotted two people walking down to the horses, stepping out of a lamp's light. It was dark out, but from the wide-brimmed hats, Spalding knew it was unmistakably the White Hand members. They stepped into the light again as they reached the stationed horses.

"Okay, you guys go around back and circle to the other side of the posts. I'll distract them with conversation."

"Nox, come," Billy said as he hurried around the other side of the hotel. Nox followed, leaving Spalding alone.

Here we go, Spalding thought as he fast-walked up to the two White Hand members. He had to think quick about what he could say to distract the pair from mounting their horses and leaving for the night. They had waited too long to mess this up.

"Hey!" Spalding called out, waving his hand as the two White Hand members began to untie their horses from the post.

Niles looked up. "What do you want, Spalding? We're not doing business anymore."

"Yeah," Spalding said as he slowed down. "About that—Bran mentioned something about talking to him if I was ever done with those Fleshers."

"Did he?" Irene said, raising an eyebrow.

Spalding looked at her. *Dammit,* Spalding thought. Her eyes were mesmerizing, putting him into a trance. He sucked himself into it. Why did she have to speak? *Snap out of it.* "Yes, Bran did. I think I'd like to have a chat with him."

Niles looked at Irene and shrugged. "Alright."

A large black shape appeared from behind the posts—Billy. It grew larger until the light cast sharp shadows over his figure, painting a sinister visual of the man. The sight of him intimidated even Spalding. He knew when Billy was in hunting mode.

Spalding looked over at Irene. That crooked nose. The dimple. The freckles. Those piercing eyes. Hypnotic.

What a shame, Spalding thought. *She's a real catch.*

Billy lunged forward and snagged Niles from behind, knife in hand.

Spalding charged Irene, grabbing both of her arms. He spun her around and put her in a chokehold before she could do anything.

"Hey!" Irene shouted.

"Keep talking, and I'll break it," Spalding whispered.

"You wouldn't dare," she hissed.

Niles had his arms up, saying nothing as he stared at Spalding.

"What's this about?" Irene asked.

Nox stepped out of the shadows, creeping up to the group. His fists were coiled, brows slanted, forming a scowl as he moved in front of Niles. "Y-y-you," the young man said.

"Spalding," Irene said softly. That voice. That velvety tone. "What is this?" she asked.

Ignore her, Spalding thought. "Billy," Spalding said. "Let's get out of the light. Too many people here."

Billy nodded and pulled on Niles to move with him. Nox followed. Spalding pushed Irene to walk with him. His shove had enough force behind it to cause her to grunt.

"You're rough in all the ways you handle a woman, aren't you?" Irene said.

"Quiet," Spalding said. "We'll keep this civil." *I hope,* Spalding thought. Truthfully, he didn't know where this was going to go. They needed to close off the possibility that Alastor's death had involved Niles.

"Spalding, what do you want?" Irene asked.

"I said quiet." Spalding squeezed her neck, causing her to gag. *Knock her out,* Spalding thought. He couldn't. He didn't want to hurt her. Spalding felt an odd sensation of pain inside him. This wasn't a normal emotion for him when he inflected violence. Irene really did have his heart.

The group moved far from the hotel and out of sight, deeper

into the forest behind the hotel. The location was discreet enough that no one would find them. Eventually, they came into a small grassy clearing in the woods where the moon was bright enough for them to see each other.

"What's this about?" Niles asked.

Nox stepped closer to him and threw a fist into his face. "T-t-tell me!"

Niles turned his face back to the young man. "I have no idea what this is about. How about you tell me before you start hitting me?"

"Spalding," Irene said. "What are you doing?"

Spalding squeezed her neck, saying, "I said quiet. I will do it."

"Okay, tough guy," Irene said.

Sass even in the darkest of times, Spalding thought. He admired that about her. He was no different.

Nox threw another fist into Nile's face. "Alastor!"

Niles spit some blood. "Alastor Flesher?" he asked.

"Y-y-yes. You killed him, didn't you?" Nox asked.

"No, I didn't do anything." Niles looked over at Spalding. "We've been through this."

"N-n-not the same," Nox said.

"We know about your son, Arnaldo," Spalding said. "We also know about your lover, Angeline."

Niles's nostrils flared, and he jerked a bit in Billy's arms. "You and Alastor killed her. My love!" he hissed. "What kind of monsters go around murdering families for money?"

"The kind that want to be paid by people like you," Spalding said. "You knew all this time that Alastor and I killed Angeline?"

Irene squinted. "Niles? You have a son?"

Niles looked to the ground.

Nox launched another fist into his face. "Answer!" he shouted.

Niles exhaled heavily. "Yes, Irene. I do. Angeline and I had a child. We didn't mean to, but God blessed us."

"G-g-god did not do anything," Nox snarled.

Niles shook his head. "My son hurried to me, crying, telling me everything that happened to Angeline and her husband. He described you and Alastor perfectly. I knew."

"A-a-and what did you do?" Nox asked.

"I tried to let it slide. Irene knows as well as I do that the Black Hand and White Hand do not talk, let alone have a romantic affair. It's too messy to mix the gangs. Angeline and I were in love, though; that was something we couldn't deny."

"I kept your damn secret for you," Irene said. "You couldn't tell me the whole thing?"

"You leveraged that just fine for your affairs," Niles shot back.

"I didn't bring us here because of them!" Irene shouted.

"Niles," Spalding said. "Why didn't you just tell us you were going to meet Alastor?"

"I couldn't," Niles said. "Just like I couldn't tell Irene about my son. For his own safety. Hell, you already tried to expose my affair to Bran. I couldn't risk my son's life."

Nox reached into his pocket and pulled out a switchblade, pointing it at Niles.

"Jesus Christ," Irene muttered. "Spalding, please." Her posture relaxed, communicating submission.

Ignore her, Spalding thought. He inhaled through his nose, picking up a whiff of her natural scent. Sweet. Calming. Everything about her melted him.

Nox stepped close to Niles and pressed the blade against his cheek. "A-a-and what did you do?"

"I had to confront Alastor about it. I couldn't keep living my life in the shadows. I set up a time to meet him."

Nox slashed the blade down, slicing the man's face. Niles let out a yelp of pain as Nox sliced the other cheek. Blood oozed down his whiskery face.

"Please!" Niles cried. "What do you want me to say?"

"Did you murder my father?' Nox shouted.

"No! Alastor never showed up. Spalding blamed Bran. Years went by with no answers. I never told anyone except Irene. Bran would have my head if he knew I had an affair with someone affiliated with the Black Hand. They've caused nothing but grief for us because of Donnie's death." The man began to whimper. "Please let me go," he begged.

"You lie," Nox said, bringing the knife to the man's face again.

"No, I swear to God. He never showed."

"Lies!" Nox shouted. "Y-y-you didn't come clean when Spalding confronted you. You're a snake."

The group fell silent; only the heavy breathing of Niles could be heard in the cold, dark night. Nox stared at him with hateful eyes. Spalding held onto Irene tightly, waiting, watching.

"HOO!" came a distant sound. An owl landed on a nearby branch, staring at the humans below.

Billy looked over at the animal, squinting.

Nox hacked the knife at the man's face again. Niles groaned in pain as the knife sliced down his cheek, causing his skin to flap against his jawline.

"Please! What do you want me to say?" Niles cried.

"Nox," Spalding said. "I th—"

"Quiet!" Nox shouted, his hair dangling in front of his face. The kid was vengeful. He was consumed by bloodlust. Seeing the wild-eyed look of the young Flesher, Spalding knew that someone was going to die tonight. Someone had to pay for Alastor's death.

"Okay! I did it! Is that what you want to hear? Please, just let me go. I have a son!" Niles cried.

Nox let out a roar, slashing the knife at Niles again. The blade sliced down his face, meeting with the endpoint of the previous slash. His cheek began to peel back, revealing the inside of his mouth.

"Christ," Irene moaned. "Who are you people?"

"Not the type of people you should know," Spalding said. *Don't talk to her!* he thought. He couldn't help it. Irene had never been exposed to this part of Spalding's life. He felt a need to be the voice of reason for her.

Niles's face squinted as blood continued to pour from his loose flesh. "Please!" he groaned. "What do you want me to say?"

Nox reached into his other coat pocket and pulled out a syringe.

No, Spalding thought. The dope.

The young man stepped closer to Niles and injected the needle into his neck, draining the syringe's fluid into his system.

Nox stared at the man for a few moments. "How d-d-does that feel, Niles? Do you feel less? But still enough? Do you have less c-c-control but can experience it all?"

"We have money!" Irene shouted. "Please, leave him. Niles,

I'm so sorry."

Nox stood still, staring at Niles as the man wept. Nox's face crunched up, and he let out a roar, charging forward. His knife plunged into Niles's stomach, slicing, then plunging in again. Niles cried in agony as about half a dozen stabs entered his body until his clothes were mangled, stained in red, and organs draped out of his body.

"Oh, God!" Irene squirmed in Spalding's arms. "Please!" she whispered to Spalding. "End this. Please."

Spalding stared blankly as Nox grabbed hold of Niles's open organs. He pulled the intestines out, stretching them upward and shoving them into Niles's mouth. This was not just revenge. This was Nox's obsession with vivisection in full force. The torture, the techniques—Nox had fantasized about the day he could blame someone for his father's death and exact revenge. Nox was blinded by rage. Not even Pierre would approve of this, Spalding knew. What would that mean for Irene?

"Spalding," Irene begged.

I can't let her die, Spalding thought. A crazy thought. What was he thinking? If she got away, she could tell Bran. She was also the one woman whom he couldn't get out of his mind. That meant something, right? Love or whatever?

"Hit me," Spalding whispered through the gurgling cries of Niles. *This is stupid. Stop.*

"What?" Irene said. "I can't move."

"I'm loosening my grip. Hit me and run. I'm so sorry," Spalding said as he loosened his grasp on the woman. *Why?*

Irene looked back at him, her eyes filled with fear. Her crooked nose, the freckles. This might be the last time he'd ever see those perfect features. After this, why would she see him again?

An elbow went flying into Spalding's jaw, knocking him back. Irene broke free from Spalding's loose grasp and darted from the open area.

"Spalding!" Billy called out.

Damn! Spalding thought. The blow to his jaw hurt a lot more than he'd expected. That girl could really throw a hit. "I got her!" Spalding said, lying.

Spalding turned around and ran after the woman, entering the forest. He stopped when he was out of sight from the clearing, out of view. Spalding wasn't going to go after her. He had already made his choice. He only had to give the illusion that he was chasing her.

This is pure chaos, Spalding thought. Seeing Nox unleash his anger had been disturbing. It was not like Alastor at all. Nox's father had had his moments of cruelty, but nothing to the extent that was witnessed today. Maybe it would be enough to keep

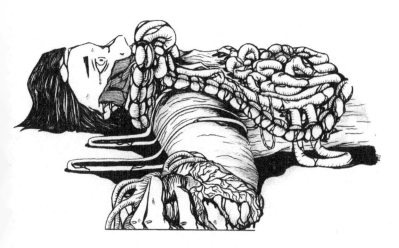

Irene quiet.

After a few minutes, Spalding returned back to the open patch where Billy stood off to the side of Niles's mutilated corpse, staring at the owl in the tree.

Niles's intestines still remained in his mouth. He didn't scream. He wiggled his fingers a bit, trying to move them. Nox stood overtop of him, knife and syringe in hand, watching as the life in Niles's eyes began to fade.

The hunt was over. The Flesher clan was presumed avenged.

ACT V

Acceptance

EPILOGUE
A NEW LIFE

"Can you bring back some bread on your way home, dear?" A soft voice floated over from the kitchen. *Dear*—a word that had become a common thing for Spalding to hear. A word that he knew from others who married. A word he only knew from short flings of lust with women who used it as part of their charm. Hearing the word *dear* from the same woman for more than a decade and a half was an entirely new concept. The word had a deeper meaning now—one of love, companionship, and care.

"Of course," Spalding called out as he put his coat on.

A redhead came around the corner, her hair tied in a bun, cooking apron on. She looked up at Spalding with her big hazelnut eyes.

Penny, my wife, Spalding thought. He thought back to when he first laid eyes on her at Walter's home, when they were both so different and young.

285

The lady leaned up and pecked Spalding on the cheek. "Thank you, dear."

"I'll be back after work," Spalding said. *Dear,* he thought. The word his wife used for him. Their marriage seemed to go by like a blink of an eye. Nox had given an odd sense of fatherly approval of their marriage when they were off to dismember Niles. Penny and Spalding hadn't spent much time together before that moment. Oddly enough, Nox seemed to play a successful cupid.

Spalding enjoyed Penny. She was blunt, strong, and as loyal as Nox had told him the Fleshers were. Hell, they even started going to church together, something Spalding had never bothered with before. The girl was oddly distant, though. Emotionally. The passion of intimacy was one trait Spalding craved. He knew that the honeymoon phase was always the peak with any relationship. Naturally, the passion and reality levelled out. He hadn't thought comfort would become so stale so quickly. The old life of unpredictability, working in the shadows, and fiery women seemed so long ago.

Irene, Spalding thought. She had burning energy that was unmatched. The girl who he couldn't get out of his mind, even after all these years. She did enter his thoughts less frequently over time. The White Hand never came by, nor did Irene. Every once in a while, he thought back to her and the confusing sense of desire and frustration he felt for her. That couldn't have been love.

"Dad!" A young girl's voice shouted. The voice shot Spalding back into the present and Irene dissolved into distant memories.

Spalding glanced over to see a young girl with dirty blonde

hair look up at him.

"Dad! Louise found a dead squirrel!" the girl said. She folded her arms in angsty teenage frustration.

"Lisa," Spalding said with a smirk. "A squirrel?"

"Yes, it's all mangled."

"Why are you telling me?" *Teenager logic.* "Go keep your sister company and make sure she doesn't do anything wild with that corpse."

Lisa rolled her eyes. "Okay," she said before rushing down the hall.

"Don't get too dirty, we just washed your dresses!" Penny called out.

"I know, Mother!' Lisa shouted back.

Oh, the times had changed. Everything had changed for the residents at Rutherford Manor. Change, the one constant. Just under two decades had welcomed many new faces arrived and birthed at the manor. Spalding couldn't keep track of them all. He had a wife and two beautiful daughters to think about. That was his focus. Plus, there was the butcher shop. His legitimate way of earning a living.

Spalding turned to give his wife a kiss on the lips. The two embraced for a moment before Spalding released her.

"I'll be home after work," Spalding said.

"Of course," Penny said with her usual closed smile.

Spalding left the manor and approached the stable where the horses were kept. The summer air was cool, as it was most mornings this early. The sun was beginning to peek over the horizon. This was the regular daily start to his life.

The carriage was just outside of the stable. A horse was

attached to it and the back door was open.

"Billy?" Spalding called out.

Billy popped around the corner with a human-sized sack hauled over his shoulder.

"That isn't one of the townsmen, is it?" Spalding asked.

Billy shook his head. "No," he said. "That was one time, two years ago."

"Mr. Connors was a good man," Spalding said. "Just making sure no other good folk go missing in Rowley."

"I know," Billy said. "That was one time. We are more careful."

"Good," Spalding said. "See you at the shop later today?"

"I'll come by after I drop these off at Nox's laboratory."

Spalding tipped his hat and wandered off to the stables to get his own horse. He did his best to keep out of Nox's business. Billy seemed to enjoy grabbing innocent lives for Mr. Flesher's experimentations. Unlike his father, Nox had a fixation with the human body. He was obsessed with torture as well. History proved so.

The less I know about what goes on down there, the better, Spalding thought. He was closer to Alastor's work than he was to Nox's. Alastor wasn't as sadistic as Nox, and Spalding had a higher tolerance for the chaos back then. Now, he wanted to keep life as simple as possible.

Spalding got on his horse and rode off from Rutherford Manor into the town of Rowley. This had been his routine for over a decade and a half. It had taken Spalding and Billy years to bring the butcher shop up to a sustainable income. The funds were nothing close to the type of cash they pulled in while working as resurrectionists, but it was peaceful and risk-free.

Simple was what he needed. What his wife and daughters needed. They had to have a loving husband and caring father figure.

A gunshot echoed through the forest, and the horse whimpered. The animal's legs collapsed as it tumbled down to the ground, skidding to a stop. The impact of the beast's mass hitting the gravel threw Spalding into the air. He collided into the road headfirst, sliding in the dirt.

His top hot flew off, somewhere. His face was bloody from the scrapes. He quickly rolled onto his back to see what had happened. Where did the shot come from?

"Shit," Spalding said while reaching into his pocket to see if he had something. He knew better; he never kept weapons. That wasn't his style.

Another shot fired, and dirt flew into the air inches from him.

"Alright!" Spalding said while raising his arms. "You got me!"

Silence.

Another shot rang out, and the dirt beside Spalding's feet sprouted up. He wiggled backwards.

"Spalding!" The male voice came from the forest.

"That's me," he said. *Who is this?*

Rustling from the nearby bushes came from the side of the road until a young, dark-haired man popped out. He had a bandana over the lower half of his face. He held a rifle in his hands, pointing it at Spalding.

"You shot my horse. That was a cruel thing to do," Spalding said.

"Shut up! You're next."

"You haven't shot me yet," Spalding said. "You have something to say."

"I do," the man said. "I've waited way too long for this moment."

"Really? Mind sharing a bit about yourself? You know enough about me, clearly."

The man used one hand to pull down his bandana, revealing a scar along his cheek.

Spalding felt his heart sink. Arnaldo. Niles' boy.

Arnaldo scowled and held the rifle with both hands, stepping closer to Spalding. "That was the face I wanted. The face of shock, even though you knew this day was coming."

"Truthfully, I wasn't sure. After all the things I've done, I was surprised nothing has come back to haunt me until now."

"I never forgot. All the terrible things you and the Fleshers have done. I know about it. My father was involved with it. You just did the dirty work. My dad tried to keep me out of it. But I know all the terrible things you've done. You're a sick fiend!"

"It was never our intention to kill your mother," Spalding said.

"Yes, it was!" Arnaldo shouted. "You needed a body to get paid by the White Hand. My family meant nothing to you! No one means anything to you!"

Spalding shook his head. "Okay, but if I had known Niles was brushing with the lady, I wouldn't have engaged. How could have we known?"

"I don't care. You killed my mother, and you killed my father too."

"That I, unfortunately, have to take credit for." Spalding sighed. "Irene tell you that?"

"She eventually found me. She told me who you were. I waited for my father to return that night. He never did."

"Lovely gal," Spalding said. "How is she?"

Arnaldo raised the rifle. "None of your fucking concern!"

"Alright, so you plan to kill me. Why haven't you?"

"I wanted to see your face. I want to see the fear in your eyes before I shoot you and finally avenge my family."

"Fair enough," Spalding said. He couldn't think of a way out of this. He was on the ground, weaponless, and had a gun pointed to his face. The kid had a good shot. Spalding could only talk his way out of this. What could he say? There wasn't much he could think of. Arnaldo obviously had been waiting for this moment for years. Perhaps Spalding was about to join Pierre in the afterlife. If there was one. If there was, there would be a lot more pissed-off people waiting for him. He'd killed a lot over the years.

"Tell me," Spalding said. "If this is my end, mind answering one last question for me?"

Arnaldo remained silent.

"Did your father kill Alastor?"

"No. He was going to meet him and confront him about my mother's death, but the man never showed."

"I was afraid so," Spalding said. "Even though your father confessed to it."

"What?" Arnaldo said.

"Yeah, I think he was trying to get Nox to stop."

"And you stood by doing nothing," Arnaldo said.

"Why'd you wait all these years to find me?" Spalding asked.

"I waited, yeah. Once I found you, I saw you were married.

Your wife was pregnant."

He knows where we live, Spalding thought.

"Ultimately I decided to wait—wait for your kids to be old enough to experience the pain I went through." Arnaldo tightened his grip on the gun. "Now they will. Go to hell Spa—"

A whizzing noise roared through the air. Blood splattered onto Arnaldo's gun and Spalding's face. The sharp, pointed end of a hatchet pierced through Arnaldo's neck. His eyes were wide. He gurgled and gasped for air. He dropped the rifle as he reached for his neck, feeling the hatchet.

Spalding hurried to his feet as the boy collapsed to his knees. Arnaldo's eyes showed disbelief, shock, and confusion as he tumbled to the ground. Blood continued to ooze out of his neck and stained the gravel below him.

"Close one," shouted the familiar monotone voice of Billy. He stood at the far end of the road, on his horse.

"My God," Spalding said, shaking his head. "You could not have timed that any better." He wiped his forehead, trying to brush off the dirt and blood.

Billy's horse trotted toward him. The man didn't even look at Spalding or the dead boy beside him. His eyes were up, looking into the trees.

Spalding looked over to see a grey owl resting on the branches, staring at them.

"What?" Spalding asked.

Billy's horse came to a stop a few meters from him. "I know that owl," Billy said.

"Yeah, me too. They have a funny way of showing up anytime something bad happens," Spalding said.

"No, not they, her."

Spalding shook his head. "Sorry?"

"Do you remember the tale of my mother and the demon, Muunat?"

"Aye," Spalding said.

Billy pointed at the owl with his index finger.

The owl flapped its wings and leaped from the branches, flying off into the distance.

"Wait," Spalding said, pointing at the bird. "I just hit my head, so you better not be fucking with me."

"No, no fucking."

"Muunat, the demon that your mother made a deal with?" *Penny mentioned Muunat, too. The fire,* Spalding thought. A grey owl had also appeared when Alastor and Spalding attacked Angeline and Donnie on the second snatch. It allowed Arnaldo to get away. "No," Spalding muttered. "It's just an owl."

"Yes, Spalding. The demon that tainted my mother's womb. The owl that was there when Nox disembowelled Niles. Muunat shapeshifts from her true form into an animal to observe. She craves chaos; she desires destruction. The same sensations I feel with my addiction."

"That owl?" Spalding said. "No way." He was a practical man who believed in what he saw in front of him. This couldn't be real.

"You're a Savdige, Spalding. You live in Rutherford Manor with the Fleshers. The spirit world is constantly around you. Are you blind?"

Spalding wiped his face. "No, I am aware of these kinds of things. I mean, Lilith has sensations all the time. But a demon?

All these years? It's just an owl. Demons have horns, don't they?"

"Muunat shapeshifts." Billy said.

"Christ." Spalding attempted to wrap his head around the number of times he'd seen the owl. The numerous occasions when an owl had conveniently showed up. Was it Muunat? The tall tale that Billy and Penny spoke of? "Alastor, he had owl feathers in his grasp."

"I remember you mentioning," Billy said.

"All this time?" Spalding said.

Billy shrugged. "I have never spoken to her or seen her true form. She only watches me. She is a being of the spirit world. Ancient, angry, and evil. She has her own agenda, orchestrating chaos."

Alastor's words echoed through Spalding's mind. *"I keep you in the dark for your own protection! I don't think you have the spirit to handle some of these unholy things."* The words Alastor spoke on their second snatch. They weren't about the resurrection business at all.

A second visual of Alastor's study rushed through Spalding's mind. Nox knocked the globe from the table. A ritual scroll complete with owl wings and demonic eyes had fallen to the ground. *Alastor. The White Hand. Donnie's family, Niles's death,* Spalding thought. *The owl was always there.*

"Perhaps Alastor followed a similar path of desperation as your mother did," Spalding said.

"How so?" Billy asked.

"We were pretty desperate, Billy. Eating people, as you know. Alastor was not afraid of trying unusual measures."

"I see."

Spalding exhaled heavily. "Lilith sensed something supernatural around Alastor's body." It was a shot in the dark, but at this point in time, Spalding was willing to throw any ideas out there. Alastor making a deal with a shapeshifting demon puppeteering death and destruction was a plausible answer.

Billy shook his head. "I was not there and can't speak the truth. I can tell you, I wouldn't be surprised. She is persuasive and always watching."

"Why didn't you mention her before? When you saw her that night with Niles?"

"Niles was already dead. Nox had made up his mind. Muunat's will was complete."

Spalding was still having a difficult time coming to terms with all of it. Twice Spalding and Nox tried to peg the White Hand for Alastor's death and ended up nowhere. Was a demon really behind all of it?

"Well," Spalding said. "How does that saying go?"

"What?" Billy said.

"That British writer, Arthur Conan Doyle."

"Never heard of him."

"He said something like, 'When you have eliminated the impossible, whatever remains, however improbable, must be the truth.'"

Billy nodded. "That would be Muunat."

Even with the shocking news, the two men still had to run their shop. Spalding could spend all day thinking about the demon-bird and what else Alastor had hidden from him. Spalding rode on the back of Billy's horse and the two trotted into town. Sadly, Spalding would have to purchase a new steed. But those were tomorrow's issues. As it was, he had a store to take care of.

The blow to his head wasn't too severe. He didn't need stitches. Thankfully, he knew how to fall in the least damaging way. Even after the shake-up with Arnaldo and the discovery of a demon-bird, Spalding stayed focused on work. He needed it. Going through such a shock made the mind-numbing task of maintaining the storefront and slicing up farm animals welcoming.

Throughout the day Spalding's mind revisited the various times he'd seen the owl demon. The number of times Muunat was around was baffling. All these years, through all the broken hearts, anger, hate, and misery, Spalding finally had an answer to what happened to Alastor. It was all part of some demon's sick plan. Something Alastor got himself involved with in an attempt to save his family. A deal between Alastor and the creature. A mysterious deal as elusive as the demon itself.

Was it over? Had Muunat finished her deed with Alastor? Or did she have future plans for those of Rutherford Manor? Billy seemed to accept the demon. He did have a deeper connection to it than anyone else. He didn't seem overly concerned.

"Don't worry," Billy said as they were closing up shop. He joined Spalding throughout the day, and they dealt with their regular customers until they could lock up and head home. "Muunat will return. She always does," he said.

"That sounds like something I should be worried about," Spalding said.

"You can fixate on the evil. Be consumed by it. Believe me, I of all people should know."

"How do you deal with it?" Spalding asked.

"I focus on what I care about in this world. Vivian helped me. You, Spalding, have a wife and two lovely daughters. Let that be your strength."

Spalding nodded. He was not entirely convinced. The thought of a supernatural evil lurking in the shadows wasn't something he could brush aside. Ignoring it and focusing only on the good was a form of naivety. Then again, what else could he do? You couldn't fist-fight a demon. Not to his knowledge.

"Let me just pick up some bread from the bakery, and we can head out," Spalding said.

"Sure," Billy said. "You know what also helps with distracting your mind?"

"What?"

"Fight club," Billy said with a grin.

"Aye, yeah," Spalding said. He completely forgot that the fight club was tonight. Something that always seemed to lighten the mood. He needed it now more than ever.

After the errand, Spalding and Billy rode out of Rowley and back to Rutherford Manor. After dinner, Spalding digested his meal on the veranda, smoking a cigarette, watching as the sun began to set. Billy and Spalding would be heading to the fight club soon.

Footsteps came from behind him. "S-s-Spalding," came Nox's voice as he stepped into view and sat down beside him. Nox looked more and more like his father with age. Spalding couldn't help but see Alastor's ghost.

"Nox," Spalding said, taking a puff from his cigarette.

"I heard about th-the incident this morning, with Niles' son."

"Yeah," Spalding said. "What did you hear?"

"He attacked you, seeking revenge."

"That sounds right. Billy saved my ass. I'd be dead if it weren't for that man."

"He's returned your favour," Nox said.

"True. Arnaldo said something to me before he died."

"Wh-wh-what?"

"I asked him about your father and his father meeting."

"Niles c-c-confessed," Nox said in a cold tone.

"Arnaldo said that never happened. He said Alastor never made it to the meetup."

"Niles was a liar. He could have lied to his son."

"I don't think so," Spalding said.

"It doesn't matter." Nox said. "Arnaldo is dead. Niles is d-d-dead. The Fleshers won in the end."

"Does that make you feel better?" Spalding asked.

"What?"

"Projecting revenge onto someone who's not guilty?"

"It gives me acceptance of the situation."

"You heard who else was there when Arnaldo showed up?"

"Billy?" Nox asked.

"And?"

Nox shook his head.

"A demon. Supposedly the one orchestrating all of this. The one who killed Alastor."

Nox snorted. "I don't buy it. That has no logic behind it."

Spalding raised an eyebrow. "If there is no logic, you don't believe in it?"

"No. Niles is the most rational explanation. It wasn't some otherworld entity that controlled the whole thing. I am sticking to that."

"Even after knowing what your father had been into in an attempt to save us from cannibalism?"

"Yes. I don't believe it."

"Or what about that scroll?"

"From my father's study? No."

Spalding let out a sigh. How was Nox so intelligent yet so narrow-minded?

Billy walked out onto the veranda and took a slight bow. "Ready?" he asked.

"Yeah," Spalding said. *I don't need to debate with Nox. He's made up his mind.* "I think a few fists will help us shrug this all off," Spalding said while tipping his hat to Nox. He could use a good ol' fight to keep his mind off of all that had happened. The fight club was the one thing he could rely on in a world of change. A world where even a stable life brought no joy. He needed a constant to ground himself, waiting, hoping Muunat wouldn't return.

THANK YOU

FOR READING THE WHITE HAND, A RUTHERFORD MANOR NOVEL!

WOULD YOU CONSIDER GIVING IT A REVIEW?

Reviewing an author's book on primary book sites such as Amazon, Kobo and Goodreads drastically help authors promote their novels and it becomes a case study for them when pursuing new endeavors. A review can be as short as a couple of sentences or up to several paragraphs, it's up to you. You can find review options for the novel on Amazon or Goodreads.

ABOUT THE AUTHOR

Konn Lavery is a Canadian author whose work has been recognized by Edmonton's top five bestseller charts and by reviewers such as Readers' Favorite, and Literary Titan.

He started writing stories at a young age while being homeschooled. After graduating from graphic design college, he began professionally pursuing his writing with his first release, Reality. He continues to write in the thriller, horror, and fantasy genres.

He balances his literary work along with his own graphic design and website development business. His visual communication skills have been transcribed into the formatting and artwork found within his publications supporting his fascination of transmedia storytelling.

45384842R00169

Made in the USA
Middletown, DE
16 May 2019